Secrets Café,
The Appetizer

by

Gina G.

This is a work of fiction. Names, characters, places, and incidents are either the product of the author's imagination or are used fictitiously, and any resemblance to actual persons living or dead, business establishments, events, or locales, is entirely coincidental.

Secrets Café, The Appetizer

COPYRIGHT © 2022 by Gina G.

Cover Art by *Diana Carlile*

The Wild Rose Press, Inc.
PO Box 708
Adams Basin, NY 14410-0708
Visit us at www.thewildrosepress.com

Publishing History
First Edition, 2023
Trade Paperback ISBN 978-1-5092-4614-4
Digital ISBN 978-1-5092-4615-1

Published in the United States of America

Dedication

To the city of Seattle, thank you for the memories.
To my friends and family, thank you for believing in
me.

Appetizer:

1. A small dish served before a meal that stimulates the appetite.
2. Something that stimulates a desire for more.

.

Chapter 1

Shh, it's a Secret

I met her at the Christmas Party. That was my first mistake. I'm not a fan of Christmas parties. I may as well tell you that right now. I'm pretty sure it has to do with the fact that I am (a) widowed, and (b) work in retail. Ever since my partner Leslie passed away, I have had to force myself to attend social situations. But Janet and Lori's party was an annual event. Normally my best friend Thomas, the reigning Queen of Seattle went with me, but on this night, he was booked elsewhere.

Janet and Lori lived in the Queen Anne neighborhood of Seattle. Their living room window framed a view of the Seattle skyline with the Space Needle holding center court. When I arrived, the party was in full swing. I nodded to several people I knew as I made my way through the crowd searching for Janet. The house was filled with the joy and color of Christmas. I glanced at my watch, thinking an hour would be acceptable before I could call an Uber and run away. Janet was in the kitchen adding spiced rum to a bowl of eggnog. She gave me a half hug. I thanked her for the invite plus the flannel shirt theme. Flannel was my idea of comfort for the holidays. Janet took me around, introduced me to a few people and that was when I saw her. She was standing at the chip bowl wearing designer jeans, a blue and green flannel shirt over a tight tank top which hugged her body in all the right places. Her ash blonde hair was styled in an asymmetrical cut, longer on one side than the other. She had the look I liked, edgy with a side of vulnerability like something inside was broken. She caught my gaze and her beautiful, caramel brown eyes flicked me up then down. I watched as she watched me watch her dip a chip into the salsa and slip it between her full pouting lips.

"I'm sorry," Janet floundered when we approached the young temptress, "I know you came with Carol, but I can't remember your name."

She put a finger to her lips, leaned in close and whispered, "Shh, it's a Secret."

I held out my hand. "I'm Georgia, nice to meet you."

I never questioned her name. I should have.

We hung around each other, lightly flirting, dancing the dance of two people attracted to each other like moths to a light, dangerous and wanting to get burned. I told her I worked at Nordstrom's as a Shoe Manager. She told me she worked on Capitol Hill and shared an apartment with roommates in the U district. At the end of the night, I took a chance, a big one for me since I rarely, if ever, ventured beyond a flirtation and asked if she would like to go out for drinks or dinner sometime.

"I guess that means you're not straight?" she winked at me.

"Bi-sexual, if you need a label." I wrapped an arm around her shoulder, holding her close as we swayed to a slow song. When she didn't say anything, I continued, hoping and praying I wasn't killing the mood. "The way I look at is, men are good for sex and women are far better for something…long term, ya know? Something more than a one night stand."

She ducked her head and looked away. "I'm not twenty-one yet," she whispered.

"Please tell me you are not seventeen," I begged, trying to make light of the situation while my heart sank, backed off and said no, don't do it.

"No, I'm twenty," she replied. "How old are you?"

I thought about lying, but I believe that honesty is always the best way to go. It just saves you so much time from having to figure out which lie you chose to cover up with which lie.

"I will be fifty in March."

"Wow." She moved in closer so I could feel the heat of her body. "You could be my mother. But much sexier."

"Thank you." I wasn't sure what else to say.

She looked into my eyes as she licked her lips. "Age doesn't matter to me." She toyed with a strand of my hair, leaned down, her lips scant inches away from mine. I could feel the heat of her breath, smell the sweat of her perfume. Her lips were inviting, whispering of intimacy. Mine were hesitant, followed by hunger and curiosity. It was the kind of moment that happens when eyes met eyes and flick to the lips. I went for it, gently kissed her and slowly tasted the softness of her.

We exchanged numbers. She texted me when I got home.

—So nice to meet you, I really, really want to see you again and get to know you better. But you have to promise me one thing. You can't tell anyone about me. #Secret.—

And that is how it began.

****

It was an odd situation from the start. For one thing she never wanted to go out in public. She liked hanging out my place. The few times I suggested going to hers, she said her messy, obnoxious roommates wouldn't understand.

"Besides, your place is so nice. It has a great view, is perfectly located, and has room for two."

My place was just off First Avenue, perfectly located between Pikes Place and Pioneer Square with a view of the bay and the Ferris Wheel on the pier. Secret texted me at work often to see when I would be home. If I suggested meeting up somewhere else, she was always busy. I didn't pay attention to it at first. I was simply happy for some alternative company, a distraction to my otherwise boring routine: go to work, come home, exercise, have a drink, and write. If she called and I was busy it didn't go well. She would whine and accuse me of not wanting to spend time with her. Rather than argue, I pushed whatever I was doing aside and made her the priority. She would come over and we would talk, which led to sharing, and sharing led to intimate feelings, which led to kissing, heavy petting and just when things were really heating up, she would leave. It was around the third or fourth week that sex came up.

On that particular night we were seated on my sofa watching a lesbian movie and paying enough attention to get turned on. She was gently stroking my arm while I waged a war within over the age difference.

"What's it like to have sex with a woman?"

I almost dropped my drink. I caught it before it spilled more than a drop. "You haven't had sex with a woman?"

She shrugged, her pretty shoulders falling up and

down in an "awe shucks, gee golly, no, I'm so innocent way." It was cute. Endearing. Sexy. *She was too young* my mind warned. *But I want her*, my libido whispered back.

She was the first woman I found myself sexually attracted to since my wife Leslie passed away ten years prior. During my ten-year hiatus of grief, work and life, I dated three men. One wanted a banker, someone to pay his way in life. The second was looking for a mommy to clean up after him. The third wanted a nurse to take care of him when he was sick or feeling down. I was not any of those. They sucked four years out of my life. I tried dating a few women, but when they started hinting about moving in on the second or third date I backed out. I hadn't dated anyone long term for the past five years.

Now, let me stop for a moment to give you just a bit of background. I am bi-sexual. Get your complaining out now. It's a simple fact. I like men and I like women but by far my best and longest relationship was with Leslie and I would still be with her to this day if she hadn't passed away. I had slept around a bit with men but that was strictly for sex. A vibrator is only good so many times and then you crave something real, actual hands to hold you, a body to lie against. It was ten years since I had been with a woman sexually and I wanted to know if I still had it in me. I wanted to know if I could still get a woman off. I wanted to know what Secret tasted like. When she said she had never been with a woman, my curiosity spiked, my desire got excited and the part of me that was worried about the age difference threw in the towel.

"Whatever could we do about that?" my voice dropped into a sexy kitten purr. The temperature in the room went up ninety degrees.

"Maybe," she whispered letting her hand brush the nape of my neck, while the other trailed down my chest and set my heart racing, "Maybe, you could teach me." And she leaned in for a kiss.

Now I ask you, just what the hell would you do? Here is this lithe, young Goddess, asking you to teach her how to make love to a woman and you haven't had pussy in how long? Do you just say oh here is a manual let me know if you have any questions? No! God no! You dive right in.

I pulled her long-sleeved shirt over her head. "First you start with the erogenous zones," I said. "You want to turn a woman on. Kissing is good, but a woman's body is like an instrument. There are so many places you can touch…" I ran my fingers lightly down her arms, "stroke…kiss…lick and nibble." My tongue trailed down her throat to her ear, nibbling at her lightly. She closed her eyes, leaned her head back, and moaned.

I undid her bra, slipped it off and traced my finger around her breasts, following with my mouth. Her back arched and her little pearl nipples hardened. I took one in my mouth, circled it with my tongue and then bit, while kneading the other one with my hand, plucking and pinching at it. I lightly teased and tasted her flesh, licking between her breasts and worked my way back up her neck, to her ear. She dug her fingers into my hair and kissed me like I was the only thing that mattered.

I undid her pants and removed them, slid off the couch and knelt before her. Her breath was coming fast, and her body was on fire. I could feel it burning with heat. I parted her legs and let my fingers run up and down her thighs. Leaning in, I kissed her again, driving my tongue into her, giving her mouth a taste of what I could do to her pussy. Her eyes closed and my fingers found her wet, wanting nether lips. I slid a finger around the clit, getting her nice and wet before gently pushing a finger inside. Just one.

"Rule number one," I whispered as I worked my finger slowly in and out of her moistness. "Always do a taste test before you go down on a woman." I drew my finger out of her warmth and sucked it. She tasted like a mix of honey and coconut juice. Smooth.

"Oh my God." She could barely breathe.

I smiled at her, licked my lips and dove in.

****

I am happy to say I still had it. I worked my magic with my fingers and my tongue. She lay back, took it and when she let herself go, it was a quick little explosion that washed over me. I wiped my face dry with my hand and gave her a few moments to catch her breath.

"Wow," she said, running a hand through my hair. "That was incredible."

It was my turn to give the awe shucks shrug. "My pleasure," I replied and got off the floor which my knees thanked me for.

She started to get dressed and looked down at her watch. "Shit! Is it really this late? I'm sorry. I have to go."

There was always next time. "It's okay."

"No, really, I'm sorry. I want to try that on you. See if I can do that." She was so eager and cute that I forgave her on the spot for having to leave. She stood up, slipped on the rest of her clothes. I watched amused, and slightly disappointed. It was a feeling I would soon learn to get used to with her.

"Text me tomorrow?" She kissed me quickly, no tongue, and was gone.

I waited a bit before going into my room, opening my little nightstand drawer, and taking out my pink vibrator which was shaped just right. I stripped out of my pants and my wet panties before I lotioned up and slipped my vibrator into my hungry pussy. It didn't take me long. I was that fired up.

****

Several weeks passed like that. I didn't know what her game was. It didn't make sense. She would come over, we would talk, make out and undress each other. She would barely touch me. Why? She wouldn't nibble my neck, my earlobe, touch my breasts, nothing. Every once in a while, she would run a finger across my panty line but there was no follow through. Once I was through with her and she had gotten what she wanted she would glance at her watch and "suddenly" need to leave. She was saying all the right things, sending me little romantic texts, songs with notes like, "this one reminded me of you."

The words were pretty, but her actions were another. It was driving me crazy. I was not a priority. I felt like a prostitute, someone she could come over and take what she wanted from, without paying. It started to bother me. Seriously bother me. The only ones I could talk to about the situation were my sisters Virginia and Carolina, who lived out of state. I wished I could talk to my best friend Thomas, but I had promised I wouldn't tell anyone about her. I'd promised to keep her a secret.

At night I found myself pacing, wondering if she was going to show up, text, or call. Was it me? Was I too old? She said age didn't matter but what if it did? I had some wrinkles by my eyes, laugh lines, a few age freckles and gray hair showing up. What if those things turned her off? At night I sat at my desk writing venting, pondering, letting the words pour out of me. I wrote down her texts, puzzled over them and searched for clues. Did she like me? She said she did, the songs said she did, but her actions said otherwise. She was a puzzle I couldn't figure out.

****

The week before my birthday I'd had enough. I was done with it. I was going to be fifty soon and I did not enjoy a little twenty-year-old treating me like a freaking prostitute. So, when she came over and started to undress, I said no.

"What's wrong?" she asked with her shirt half unbuttoned.

"You owe me one, well actually more than one."

"What?"

"Sex darling. An orgasm. You do know what that is don't you?" I could not disguise the sarcasm.

She glanced at her watch. "I don't really have time."

"Let me get this right, you have time for me to get you off, but not time to return the favor? Is that what you are saying?" I kept my voice level, but my eyes narrowed.

She wasn't prepared for my anger. I wasn't quite prepared for it either.

"This is getting old," I fired the words at her.

"What?" She took a step back.

"Just what am I to you? You come over when you like, take what you want, and leave. Am I nothing to you? You don't even touch me. Are you straight? Confused about your sexuality?" I walked into the kitchen and poured myself a shot of whiskey. "If you truly cared about me, you would go out with me in public."

"I don't—"

"Oh spare me the crap about people seeing. Are you ashamed of me?"

"No, I just…I just…I'm not ready."

"Bullshit."

"Georgia—"

"No." I shook my head, I was done. "Get out. Until you can come back here and treat me like an equal, I don't want to see you. Got it?"

I pointed to the door. She stared at me for a moment like she was stunned and couldn't figure out what to say. I tapped my foot and waited. I may have appeared calm on the outside but inside I was raging. My fury crackled like a bullwhip between us. She opened her mouth, closed it, narrowed her eyes for a fraction of a second before shifting them to a downcast puppy look and slunk out the door. I followed behind her and locked it. I took my phone out and blocked her number. I wanted her out of my life. I went back in the kitchen and poured myself another shot with shaky hands watching storm clouds roll across Elliot Bay, and the sky ignite with lightening. I heard the rolling rumble of thunder before the rain threw thick drops against my window, streaking it and obscuring my view.

Chapter 2

Shh…listen

My sisters Virginia and Carolina flew me to Vegas for my fiftieth birthday. They were both married and happy to get away from the family life. My brother Tennessee had wanted to join us but couldn't. And yes, our parents named us after States. They met me at the Vegas airport and we checked in to the Paris Hotel before hitting the town. We went to a couple shows to celebrate my crossing the line into Menopause. We drank, danced, laughed, cried, shopped, gambled a bit and went bar hopping. I did everything I could to keep Secret out of my mind. Virginia challenged me to a drinking game, that every time I brought her up, I had to do a shot. I was drunk within an hour. She was like an anchor dragging our fun down at odd moments.

"I'm just mad at myself for falling for her crap," I whined.

"I think she put a spell on you." Carolina pointed a finger at me as she held her wine glass. We were back in my room at the Paris Hotel.

"Ask yourself this." Virginia rolled over on the bed and pushed her glasses back. "Is she worth it?"

I didn't want to answer the question.

Virginia and Carolina both stared at me, waiting for a reply.

I hung my head.

"She poisoned you somehow." Virginia polished her drink off.

"With words." I rested my chin on my hands. "All of her pretty words. Do you know how long it has been since anyone said stuff like that to me? Romantic stuff?" The alcohol made me want to cry.

"I think the words were a trap." Carolina got off the bed and filled all of our glasses full. "I think you need to get out of the trap."

"I think she needs to get laid." Virginia giggled. I glared at her, but we toasted regardless. The rest of the night was a blur of alcohol, neon lights and laughter.

I woke up the next morning with a wonderfully handsome young man lying next to me. He was a delicious surprise. He heard me stir and rolled over. He was not as surprised as I was. But he smiled, and his body said good morning in just the right way to leave me feeling incredibly young and sexy and reminded me I was still a woman. I was still wanted. I was still hot. He was delicious. I wondered which of my sisters I needed to thank for the handsome gift. I suspected Virginia.

My sisters dropped me off at the airport and I took the short flight home. I was in that strange place of too much sex mixed with too much to drink mixed with too much fun and not enough sleep. The plane ride was agony. Thomas picked me up at the airport, looking debonair as always in a cream-colored linen suit with a red silk tank and ruby studs in his ears. His dark skin gleamed like a polished tiger's eye gemstone. We drove to Secrets Café for a Bloody Mary.

"So? How was it?" he asked.

"How do I look?" I replied.

"Like shit." He threw his head back laughing manically.

"You are lucky I love you." I covered my ears trying to drown out his cackle. Thomas was one of my oldest and dearest friends.

We carried our drinks out to the patio. I sat gingerly down, still sore from the three orgasms Mr. Strange had gifted me with. I filled Thomas in on everything, and I do mean everything. He was peeved I hadn't shared from the beginning.

He crossed his arms. "I knew something was going on."

"What can I say? I promised I wouldn't tell."

"It's just sad." He waved a hand dismissively at me. "You know if it was love she wouldn't have asked you to keep your mouth shut. She wouldn't have made you lock yourself away. She would have been proud and happy to be out with you."

"I hate when you are right." My head was pounding.

"You deserve better Georgia."

By the time I got to my apartment, I wanted to do nothing more than crawl into bed and sleep. Pouring myself a glass of water, I took two aspirin, brushed my teeth, and stripped down to just my panties and an oversized shirt. I was about to get my wish when I heard a knock at the door. Groaning, I opened it.

Secret stood there. I didn't know what to think. She looked me up, down, took in my attire and pushed past me. I shut the door. What else was I going to do? Stand there half-naked and wait for one of my neighbors to walk by?

"Where were you?" Her voice was casual.

"Vegas." I drew the word out.

"What did you do?" She kept her eyes down.

"Well, you know…what happens in Vegas stays in Vegas right?"

"Please, tell me." Biting her lower lip, she raised her eyes to mine.

"Why? It's none of your business." I wanted the words to sound harsh, mean but they came out tired. Why was she here? Just seeing her again brought back feelings I wanted to squash and lock away.

"Georgia…" a lock of hair fell in front of her eyes.

"What are you doing here?" I asked.

"I wanted to wish you happy birthday and you weren't answering my calls."

"I blocked you." I waved my hand dismissively.

She nodded, as if assimilating, processing the information, and reached for my hand. I let her take it, hold it, feeling the familiarity of her fingers. Damn her to hell, I still wanted her. She stared into my eyes, not speaking, licked her lips and led me to the couch. She let her fingers trace the collar of my shirt and slowly started unbuttoning. She brushed her lips soft against mine, tentative, like she was testing the waters to see if I would bolt. Her fingers worked their way from my breasts to my still aching pussy. She pushed the panties aside and eased a finger in. It was the first time she had touched me in an intimate, unhurried way, like she knew what she was doing.

"I missed you," she whispered and moved her finger in and out slowly, then in circles. Her thumb found my clit. I closed my eyes and relaxed into the sensation of a woman touching me. Of *Secret* touching me, her fingers inside me, first one, then two, and it was tight but oh, it felt so good. She eased me back on the couch, hovered over me and spread my legs further apart. She knelt between them, kept the rhythm of her fingers up and added the heat of her tongue. I groaned and grasped at the edge of the couch. My hips started to move, my body closed down to everything but the sensation of her fingers, of the touch, the flick of her tongue, the suckling of her mouth and it was so close, it was right there. She scissored her fingers on the outside adding pressure to the clit and I hadn't taught her that. She kept the pressure up, kept the strokes up, let me build and build. The intensity of it added to the three prior orgasms and sent me over the edge. I gushed. The force of it pushed her hand out. It was like a shove of liquid. A release.

"Holy shit!" I lay back on the couch feeling waves roll through me.

"Are you okay?" She wiped her hands on my shirt and went into the bathroom.

"Yeah, I'm fine. A bit spent." I drew my shirt about me and slowly sat up. Once I could stand, I would need a towel. I slipped a hand between my legs, marveling at the wetness. It had been ages since that happened, and I'd been buzzed the first time. Of course, I was pretty buzzed now—but still. I hoped it wouldn't stain my couch.

She came back into the room, lifted my chin to her face and kissed me. "I'm sorry, but I have to go," her voice was soft, eyes downcast, "Please forgive me. Let me back into your life."

And just like that she was gone.

****

Secret, damn Secret, slipping in and out of my life whenever she wanted, treating me to stone cold silence that hurt and then coming back. It was like a roller coaster. I wanted her, but I wanted more, and I knew in my heart she wasn't going to give it to me.

"I was just scared," she explained later. "You are the first woman I have been with, and I didn't want to let you down."

It almost made sense. We made a pledge to be exclusive to each other. She promised we could go out and do things in public. We never did. She just came over to my place and hung out. We talked and talked and had sex. Mostly I pleased her, although she did give me at least two orgasms one of them courtesy of my vibrator. March passed into April, April into May and summer arrived.

"I'm going to Disneyland with some friends next week," she announced one afternoon

"Sounds fun." We were seated on my balcony, watching the people below as they headed to a Mariners game.

"It's for my birthday."

"Nice. Maybe when you get back, I can give you the same present you gave me." I remembered the return from Vegas orgasm.

"I was thinking…" She bit her lip and looked away, "I was thinking we could go out and celebrate my twenty-first birthday."

Go out? In public? Be still my heart. Maybe she was serious? I restrained myself from getting too excited.

"How long will you be gone?" I lightly ran a finger across her forearm.

"Five days." She replied.

A week later she left with promises to text me— about how bored she was and how much she missed me.

She did text once to tell me she had forgotten her

charger. Who did that? Who goes away and forgets their phone charger?

I let it go. She was young. It could happen. I spent the time working and writing. I caught up with Thomas, who was in between show engagements as his alter ego Karina Fire.

"I can't believe you are back with her." He rolled his eyes, and lightly patted his short dark hair with one hand

We were at The Five Points Café having lunch. It was my day off and I had wanted to go to the Chihuly Exhibit near the Space Needle. Summertime and Seattle were like lovers walking hand in hand and I was feeling poetic, full of smiles.

"When did you hear from her last?" Thomas asked.

"I told you already, she texted me the day she arrived about how she forgot her charger."

"Interesting." He bit down on his burger. I waited. "Isn't it odd how she is with friends and not one of them has a charger she can borrow?"

I chose to ignore that thought at the time. But it did eat at the back of my mind, lingering there like a dark spot on a white page. I had no contact with her. Nothing.

Thomas and I walked through the Exhibit. It was the kind of thing I wished I could share with her. I wanted her reaction. I wanted to get to know her outside of my home. I wanted to know what she liked and disliked.

"I worry about you," Thomas said, as we stood outside looking at the Space Needle.

"Me? Why?" I kept my voice light.

"I think she's using you."

"Thomas…"

"No, I'm serious. I don't want you to get hurt again. You tend to pick these people that will hurt you, break your heart. It's like you are punishing yourself and you shouldn't be."

He may have been right. There was something off. I could sense it.

Silence descended upon me. I waited. She came back Sunday and didn't text. I didn't either. I waited. Monday was the same. Tuesday, nothing. My chest was starting to hurt, and the doubts were creeping in. The voices in my head said it was all a lie, she was really seeing someone else. I didn't want to over think, over dramatize, or even give the voices in my head credit so I shut them all down and went on auto pilot.

Wednesday, I got a text.

—I think we should just be friends.—

I stared at the words for a moment letting them settle. My heart tripped, my stomach caved, and I got that feeling you get, the one where everything is falling apart, and panic is blossoming at the corners. The one where you feel like you can't breathe because it will give you away.

I sat at my desk in the stockroom and went cold. It had all been a lie. I was a fool. An idiot. I should have known better. But we had exchanged the dreaded L-word, the one with flowers and candy and rainbows flying out of unicorns butts. The one that was all consuming, promising, and filled with fairy tales that didn't exist. I wanted to bang my head down on my desk, take my heart and lock it far away. I wanted to send it somewhere so it could learn to make better choices.

I set the phone down and stood up. Walking was a daze, but it was something to do. I stumbled through the rest of my shift, responding correctly when spoken to, but screaming at myself on the inside. I was surprised no one could see the falling apart.

I called Thomas the minute I stepped onto Fifth Avenue. "You were right," I said when he answered and burst into sobs.

"Where are you?" he asked.

I choked out a reply and he agreed to meet me at Secrets. I turned right onto Union Street, wove my way between the crowds, pushed through the doors of Secrets Café and sat down at a table. Elan, the waitress with the shaved head took my order. It came out mechanical; I was on auto pilot.

I took out my notebook, my pen, and spilled my issues onto the page. I yelled at myself, called myself names, threatened my heart, told myself I would never fall in love again or trust anyone again. It seemed like a fair thing to do.

Thomas lowered his sunglasses when he walked in, stood at the entrance for a moment, found me and strutted over. "Spill it," he demanded, as he swept his purple flowy scarf over one shoulder and sat down.

I did.

He waited, assimilating the news.

"I'm just going to say it again." He crossed his legs. "Stop picking losers, Georgia. You are searching for Leslie and only finding fragments of her. Secret had her mystery, idiot number one had her cockiness, idiot number two her bravado and idiot number three, her sense of humor. It has to stop. You can't keep blaming yourself, punishing yourself, locking yourself away. You need to forgive yourself and live. We all loved her, and she is gone. Hard as it is, we all have to let her go and move on. You most of all."

"But Secret—"

"Shh, listen," He held up his hand, "I don't want to hear it. She was a waste of your time. You deserve better."

And he was right. I had set my standards too low.

I went home that night and worked out. I still hadn't responded and from Secret's silence she didn't seem fazed by it. I thought about what to say. I took out my notebook and wrote several different replies from a scathing "how could you hurt me like this" to a harsh "what the fuck" to an accusatory "who are you seeing and how long has this been going on." I didn't send any of them. I finally decided to take the high road. It was what I did best. I let it go and didn't reply.

Summer faded into fall. I spent my days at work and my nights drinking or writing. I drowned in self-help books, exercised, walked a lot, and rediscovered myself. I started falling in love with the little things: Pikes Place in the morning, the smell of coffee, old bookstores stocked to the ceiling, and the sound of the rain. Seattle became my lover and Secret was pushed to the farthest corner of my mind where I stored bad mistakes. I dared to venture out of my solitude and went to a Mariners game, a Seahawks game, a concert and even took myself out to the theater. I went on two dates with a friend of a friend named Diana. She was nice; we had similar interests and bonus of bonuses she was my age.

September rolled in with brightly colored leaves and I started to write more, little scenarios, little ideas. I would pick out people, create a character, a situation and write short little exercises. I settled into a routine: wake up, work out, stop at Secrets Café for coffee and write, go to work, meet up with friends or co-workers if they were available, go home and write. Writing helped me heal, helped me move on. I was feeling pretty good about myself. Until last night....

I was at my desk puzzling through a scene when a knock at the door interrupted my concentration.

I thought it was Thomas.

Instead, it was Secret.

She walked past me like she lived there: sat down on the couch, unwrapped a red scarf that looked like it was trying to strangle her, and smiled up at me. I felt the safe little bubble I had been living in squeeze tight.

"I missed you." She patted the cushion next to her.

I glared and said nothing. She drew in a breath, pursed her lips, and started with a packet of lies, leading to more lies, telling me she was wrong, begging me to take her back, give her another chance. It was all bullshit. I let her ramble on. It was mildly entertaining and then she dropped the bomb. My world went black. I listened, I heard it, but I was screaming inside.

When she finally stopped, I nodded, found my voice, and opened the door. "Get the fuck out of my house."

"But—"

"Now."

She tried for tears.

"Oh, give it up. I want nothing to do with you. Get out of my house or I will call the cops and have you removed." I was shaking.

For a moment I thought she was going to call my bluff, but she didn't. She gathered herself up, and with her eyes brewing a storm stopped at the doorway to look at me. With a low edged voice she said, "You'll regret this."

"I regret ever meeting you." I slammed the door shut

in her face, locking it.

I had been stupid once, I was not going to be stupid or desperate again. I got a text from her begging, pleading, another telling me what a waste I was and a third saying she would never forgive me. I ignored them all, drank a shot of whiskey, and went to bed.

There was another text from her when I woke up telling me I shouldn't ignore her. Whatever. I ignored her and got ready for work.

I stopped in at Secret's for my morning cup of coffee. It was Thursday, two weeks before Thanksgiving. The weather was in one of its rare forms, cloudy with patches of blue. I ordered a coffee with a Hawaiian twist from the handsome barista Todd. He was young with the softest brown eyes, like a cows, large and gentle. There was a story idea floating around me. I could feel it but hadn't caught it yet. I thanked him for the coffee, turned to find a table, and almost bumped into a dark-haired woman in a red scarf wearing oversized sunglasses. I apologized. She said nothing and pushed past me. I found a table near the patio door, sat down, and took out my notebook. I tapped my pen against the paper and started with a description.

Sunlight filtered through the veins of trees casting spider webbed shadows on the ground. The man sat alone; his newspaper was laid out on the table before him. There was a nervous twitchy air about him, like he wanted to be there and wanted to run away at the same time. His eyes couldn't seem to stay focused on one thing. The door to the patio opened, a tall, leggy woman wearing a red scarf and carrying a coffee loaded with cream—

My phone buzzed. I swiped it to life. It was another

message from Secret.

—*You should watch out.*—

Really? Was that supposed to scare me? I shook my head, deleted it. I wished I had never met her. I wished I could go back and relive the entire wasted year I spent on her. I wished there was a rewind button on life or at least an alarm that would go off whenever you came into contact with someone who was going to suck your soul dry.

Wait...I sat up straight in my chair. Suck you dry...vampires...but not the blood sucking kind, more of the soul sucking kind. How do you pay back an emotional vampire?

Ahh, and the idea landed, a smile grew; a delightful, evil, Cheshire cat smile. I could pay back all the narcissistic assholes who had ever fucked with me. I would write a story and roll all of those mistakes into one character. Words were a mighty weapon. If I could do it the right way, all those narcissistic users would think the story was about them and parts of it could be. Wasn't that the beauty of writing what you know? I would use the characters I had been creating, have them all affected by one single wrecking ball in some way or another. I would pick one main thing to weave through the stories, tying them together like a scarf. Or a place where they all hung out. I would write my payback and I would start with her. I felt like a magician as I picked up my pen, held it over the page and started with a simple line.

He met her at the Christmas Party.

Chapter 3

Secret Breakfast

Mike Hadley stood in line waiting to place his order. He had been coming to Secret's Café on a regular basis for the past three months. It was all his sister's fault. She told him about the place, the setting, and the coffee. Mike considered good coffee a luxury. Secret's Café did not disappoint. They had some sort of special brew, a special mix that went into their coffee and even some of their alcoholic beverages. It was what kept the regulars coming back for more. Well, that, the music, and the ambiance. Mike kept his visits to the weekends when he wasn't working. He had requested this Friday off though because his sister was coming to town. She was back from her hiatus, her recovery, if you could call staying with their parents a recovery.

"Caramel macchiato, tall, right?" The barista, wearing a name badge identifying him as Todd, asked.

"Yes please." Mike tucked his newspaper under his arm and took out his wallet.

"Anything else today?"

"One of your blueberry scones please."

Todd handed him a scone on a plate with a napkin. Mike gave him a ten, took the change and deposited a couple dollars in the tip jar before heading to the patio area outside. He was searching for a woman in a red scarf. He had specifically requested a dark haired woman with red painted lips wearing a red scarf to be seated outside with a cup of coffee loaded high with cream and a banana. This was his second reply from the ad he had put out in *The Stranger*.

Standing in the outside area, Mike adjusted his coat, and noticed the woman seated at the far table as per his request. He took the table across from her, set his plate with the scone on it down, and placed the napkin across his lap. He checked the few patrons nearby to make sure they couldn't see anything, opened his newspaper, shifted in his chair, and gave her the briefest, barest, hardly even noticeable, nods.

The woman blew on her fingers and wrapped them around the warm cup. She let her tongue slowly lick around her red painted lips before trailing it across the mound of cream. Drawing a dollop into her mouth, she closed her eyes, savoring the taste. She let her tongue circle around the straw before gently, slowly sucking in some coffee. One finger wiped at the corner of her mouth, and she licked it before setting the cup down to pick up the banana. With her fingers, she peeled the banana skin a little over half way down, exposing the pale phallic fruit. She dipped a finger into the cream and smeared a dollop on top of the banana. Some of it started to slip down the side and she ran her tongue after it, gently scooping it up and nibbling ever so delicately at the white flesh. Once she controlled the drip she took the cream that was still on her finger and sucked it off, moving her finger tantalizingly in and out of her mouth.

Mike undid his fly.

She didn't look at him.

She poised her red delicious lips over the pale firm

flesh and went down on the banana. She slipped it in, to the peel point then pulled it back out and licked along both sides. She twirled her tongue around the tip, circling it and then teasing the tip.

He reached in his pants and set his erection free. He wrapped a hand around it and felt his hardness, his need. He watched her as she worked the banana shaft in and out, in and out of her mouth. *Red lips on white flesh.*

She took another dollop of cream, a bigger one, and smeared it on top, licking up and down the shaft, tasting the cream, before swallowing the banana. She cupped it in her hands and peeled the skin all the way to the end.

He worked his hands up and down, matching the movements of her mouth, imagining red painted lips on his cock, long fingers wrapped around him, cupping his balls, holding him. He could almost feel it…He watched her, and she was good but not the same as the real thing, as the memory he played back in his mind, the one he wished he could go back to and relive. It was just a tease.

She stroked the banana.

He stroked his penis.

She licked the banana.

He stroked his penis.

She went down on the banana.

He worked himself faster and she matched him, almost seeming to moan, her eyes closed as she thrust the banana in, then out, then in. Her lips left faint pink smears, the cream a moist trail of whiteness and just like that he came. He covered it up with the napkin and bit back the cries that wanted to come forth. He regarded her and she looked up meeting his eyes. He nodded. She nodded back, flipped her long dark hair over one shoulder and ate the banana.

Mike didn't want to watch her teeth break into the phallic flesh of his imagining. He glanced around the area to see if anyone had been watching, used his napkin to clean himself up, wadded it into a ball and set it next to the plate. He zipped his pants up and sipped his coffee. It was lukewarm now. He nibbled at the scone so the staff wouldn't think it had been wasted, gathered himself together and withdrew his wallet. He took a hundred dollar bill out and folded it in the newspaper. He put his overcoat on, picked up his mug of coffee, took another sip to calm himself and walked past. Without saying a word, he set the money and the paper down in front of her and walked away.

He didn't know who she was. He didn't know what she did. He didn't care. This was the second time he had paid her to eat something suggestively. It satisfied a need and was as close as he dared to get to what he really wanted. He walked out the front door and down the street.

Mike was partially disgusted with himself. For months now he had been paying people to act out his mind warp of a fantasy, his memory of the past. It wasn't the same. They could wear a red dress, paint their lips, put on a wig, and eat a banana but no matter what, it did not match up to his dream. This was what he had been reduced to. It needed to change. And why not? He could do it. His divorce was final! His harpy of an ex no longer had any control over him! He could finally do what he wanted and be who he really was! Maybe.

Mike had spent so many years hiding his true desires that he didn't know if he dared act on them. What he needed was courage. What he needed was his sister, someone to talk to, tell the truth to.

He glanced down at his watch. Jennie would be arriving around noon, which gave him enough time to set things up at his condo for her. He wanted the room to look good, to be welcoming. He was going to get her some flowers and make it look like a hotel room with a turndown service. It would make her laugh and God knew she needed to laugh after what she had been through. He would work on getting the nerve to overcome his fears later. Right now, his sister mattered more and he wanted to make sure she was happy.

He didn't think any more about his breakfast release. It was over and done with. Already he was moving on. Besides, he had gotten what he wanted. Or close to it. Thank God the woman had worn a red scarf. It helped with the image. A bit.

Secret Rant

I don't know who he is, but if he wants to pay me a hundred dollars just to eat a banana, fine. Easy money. I know where he works though; I followed him last week. Wonder if he's a grunt or someone higher up? From the looks of the overcoat, he likes to hide behind, he has money. If he can peel off a hundred dollars just to watch me eat...what else could I get from him?

Chapter 4

Secret Beginnings

Elan Dubois stormed into Secrets Cafe like a hurricane. She removed her headphones and the music blared, echoing through the kitchen before she turned her phone off. She hurriedly hung her coat and hat up, grabbed an apron, threw it on, and picked up a tray. Her phone buzzed with a message. She pulled it out, glared at the screen and hit delete. Then shoved it back in her pocket before she rushed to the main floor. Elan gave Todd a quick look, mouthed an apology, and started to clean up the tables. She wove in and out of the patrons, smiled at the regulars, and willed her mind to forget the words stabbed in her heart.

The words had left a deep piercing wound. But Elan wasn't going to dwell on it. She gathered up the empty plates, mugs, and utensils, and wiped down the tables. It was mindless work, but it kept her busy.

She took the first load back to the kitchen and loaded up the dishwasher before going back to get the area outside. She passed by the mystery woman who was seated at her usual table writing in a notebook, eyes focused on the page, pen spilling words onto paper, her red hair an out-of-control fire covering half her face. The woman always ordered a plain coffee with a splash of coconut and macadamia nut flavoring. When Elan checked on her, she ordered a second one. Elan brought it to her before moving outside to the patio area.

Fall was her favorite time of year. She loved it. The chill in the air, the colors of the leaves, the way it felt, brisk, crisp, like leaves crunching underfoot. She loved football, Halloween, and Thanksgiving. She loved sweaters, boots, and long jackets. And damnit all, she loved Jess. Mad as Elan was at her, she still loved Jess. Maybe that was why Elan hurt so much inside. She shook her head and tried to block Jess out of her mind.

Elan concentrated on picking up the outside area. Someone had left a red scarf. She tossed it over her shoulder, wiped the table down, and picked up the newspaper lying on the next table. It must have belonged to the tall quiet man who came in almost every Saturday and ordered a caramel macchiato. He'd left a napkin on his plate covered in something sticky. Yuck, must have spilled his drink. People. She cleared off the utensils and headed back to the kitchen.

The line was dying down, which was a good thing. She hung the scarf on the back wall by her coat, loaded the dishwasher, started it up, and took a clean set of plates to the bar area where Junie could get to them.

"That's the third time this month," her boss, Eli said when she came within earshot.

Elan ducked her head. "I know. I'm sorry Eli, really. I'm sorry."

"It's your paycheck," he pointed out.

"Can I make it up?" She was thinking of her meager supplies at home.

"You can stay till eight tonight."

"No problem." She didn't have a date anyway. Shayla had taken Jess. Elan had nothing, nothing going on. Nothing.

Eli was satisfied. "Get your head back together. We have to get ready for the afternoon crowd." He clapped his hands and beamed. "Let's move people!" He was the only boss she had ever worked for who never seemed to tire. She often wondered if he was on drugs. But other than his energy, he showed no signs of addiction. He was just naturally tireless.

She finished stocking the shelves behind the bar and the combo barista area up, before she returned to the kitchen. The morning rush was easy to take care of. They were happy with muffins, donuts, fruit, and yogurt. The afternoon crowd was offered sandwiches, soups, and salads. Elan liked working in the kitchen: it was mechanical all the chopping, prepping and slicing. Unfortunately, it did not keep her from thinking about Jess.

****

Jess. Jessica Stone. Elan remembered the first time they met. Jess had been in line for an espresso and Elan had been unable to take her eyes off Jess.

There was this shy yet confidant aura about the woman dressed in a loose Seahawks tank over denim shorts with legs to die for, muscular and toned but not too defined. Elan wanted to touch those legs, to see how they felt. She stood with the broom in her hand like a forgotten appendage and practically dropped her jaw. Jess reached a hand up, removed her ball cap, and shook out her long brown hair; it shimmered like whiskey in a glass. Her hazel eyes looked green in the light thanks to the jersey. Elan wanted to touch her hair, to feel its silky texture.

Todd nudged her as he went past. "You're staring."

She picked her jaw up and was about to reply when the woman she would learn was named Jess glanced over at Elan and smiled.

Elan, who was never one to be afraid or nervous walked right over to Jess, held out her hand and said "Hi, I'm sorry if I was rude for staring at you. But you have got to be the most intriguing woman I have seen in a long time."

Jess laughed, shook her hand, and replied, "Intriguing hmm? Thank you. I'm Jess, Jess Stone."

"Elan Dubois."

"Ellen?"

"No, its French, pronounced E—lawn." Their hands remained held and a shiver ran through Elan's body, like a magical electric shock. They stared at each other. They were the same height, eye to eye, smile to smile. The line moved forward, the spell was broken, and they let go.

Elan asked her out to a Mariners game for the upcoming weekend. Jess was down for it. Their first kiss happened while the home run winning hitter ran around the bases. Fireworks went off and it was every bit the first kiss Elan always dreamed of, tentative at first and then hungry. They were perfect except for one small thing: Jess's roommate Shayla. Elan never met the woman in person. It was enough to put up with her numerous phone calls, her interruptions, and the many times Jess would glance down at her watch and say she needed to leave or Shayla would be upset. Shayla was one of those girls who needed constant attention. She and Jess had been friends since high school. Shayla was a pain in the ass as far as Elan was concerned. Elan didn't trust her. It was a gut instinct.

Regardless of Shayla's interruptions, things moved

along smoothly until first thing this morning when her phone woke her up. Elan thumbed it to life and mumbled a hello.

"Is this Elan?"

She didn't recognize the voice. "Yes."

"This is Shayla. Jess may have told you about me? I'm her girlfriend," she drew the word girlfriend out. Elan didn't say anything. The voice continued, "I know she has been seeing you for a while and I figured it was high time we let you in on the game." Shayla paused, "See, we take turns seeing other people so we can keep our relationship fresh. Kind of livens up the whole make up sex thing if you know what I mean." She laughed.

Elan swallowed, "I—"

"It's okay if you didn't know. I was just getting tired of calling Jess every time you two were out. So I thought I would let you in on the situation. This way maybe we can advance to a threesome if you are interested. Jess says you are pretty good."

All thought left Elan's mind. She couldn't even speak. She simply hung up the phone and sat for a bit trying to comprehend what had just happened. The whole relationship with Jess had been a joke? Seriously? Jess was just using her? Toying with her?

It hurt. It was an old pain brought back to life, the being pushed aside and told she didn't matter. It was echoes of a past Elan had been trying to get over ever since she left home at sixteen. Not that leaving had been an option. The horrible people who birthed her basically kicked her out, changed the locks, and sent her on her way. She lived with friends for a couple of years before running off to Seattle. Life toughened her and molded her. She learned there was only one person she could truly trust and that was herself. Well, herself, Eli, and Todd. Eli had been nice enough to take one look at scrawny, skinny, eighteen-year-old Elan and give her a job. He even let her have a room upstairs in one of his apartments until she finally got into a place of her own by Pioneer Square. Eli became the father she never really had and Todd her brother. It took her a few months to totally open up and trust then both, but now here she was, four years later and her trust, her fragile thought of falling in love, had been shattered. Love was bullshit.

To think she almost told Jess she was in love with her. Elan still felt she loved her. Jess was the first woman Elan dated and got to know, that she wanted—*wanted*—to have a relationship with. Jess was the first woman Elan felt right with, like she could be with Jess for the rest of her life.

Elan wiped a tear from her eye. She had been blindsided. She had been dreaming of how nice it would be to ask Jess to move in, and all the while Jess was having sex with her bimbo, fucked-up, piece-of-shit roommate.

She slammed a plate down.

"Whoa!" Todd exclaimed as he came around the corner. He put his hands up in mock defense. She glared at him. "Are you okay?" He asked, tugging at his beard.

"Fine." Her reply was brisk and quick.

"Liar," he replied. "What's going on?"

She let out a heavy, defeated sigh. "I found out Jess has been having sex with Shayla."

"Her best friend from high school?"

"Yeah."

"Ah, that explains your mood."

"Todd." She glared daggers at him hoping he would

leave her to wallow in her misery.

He was unfazed. "Is that why you were late."

"Yes, the bitch of a roommate called to let me in on their fun and games."

"The roommate called you. Not Jess?" He leaned against the counter, took a dish from the rack, and started to dry it. "Interesting, hmm. How many times did the roommate interrupt your dates? She was clearly jealous. And she suddenly calls you out of the blue. Think about it."

Elan stood with a knife in her hand posed over a tomato, a ripe red tomato, and thought back to all the times Jess cancelled dates because of Shayla. Elan realized she always knew there was a possibility they were having sex.

"Shit! Fuck! Damn!" She slammed the knife into the tomato, impaling it to the cutting board, oblivious to the blood red juice and pulp bleeding, oozing, spilling out.

Todd stepped back. "Whoa…"

She walked in a circle and put her hands on her hips. "She said she wanted to clue me in. Said Jess had led me on for long enough and it was time for me to know. Something like that."

Her chest felt small and tightly constricted as if her soul was being wrung between two hands. "Shit Todd, I really liked this girl. I could actually see us growing old together. To find out the whole thing was just a fucked-up game?" Elan turned her back to him. "I thought we had something. Hell, I actually started to believe we might be in love." She was not going to cry.

"Live and learn right?" Todd's voice was soft.

"Todd…" She did not want to break down.

"I know, I know. Trust me, I have made mistakes. I

know how it goes and I know how you feel about her."

Elan sighed. "I was seriously falling for her."

"I could see that."

"I can't believe she used me." She scowled.

"Who? Jess or the roommate?" Todd asked. "Have you met this Shayla chick? I don't think I have."

"No, I've never met her. I don't even know what she looks like."

"So, I've never met her either." He tugged at his beard again, thinking. "You know it's strange to me that you heard this from Shayla and not Jess. Did you call Jess or talk to her?"

"What? Call her? No." Elan had ignored all the calls from Jess. Elan hadn't listened to any of the messages and had erased the texts without reading them. Why should she read them? They would just be more lies.

"Look, I don't know what really happened, and neither do you. I just don't want to see you hurt. So, I just have one question," he said.

"Okay." She was leery.

"If she was to walk through the door right now...would you talk to her?"

"No." She was pouting, she was angry. "Maybe...yes."

"Which is it?"

"I don't know." A tear escaped, and she wiped it away. "I don't want to be hurt."

Todd nodded his head, like it was an acceptable answer. "Okay, no one wants to be hurt but let me ask you this. How do you feel about her? Truthfully?"

She didn't want to reply, but it was Todd, and he was family. She kept her eyes down. "She was the first woman I thought I could trust. It scared the crap out of me Todd, honest. That call made me feel like my heart was stabbed, nailed to a wall."

He nodded. "I understand."

"She hurt me." Elan whimpered.

"Love hurts."

"What do you think I should do?"

"Talk to her."

"What?" Elan threw her hands up, "You want me to call her?"

"No." He watched her closely. "She's out front. She wants to talk to you."

"What?" Her hands dropped, her mouth went dry, and she swallowed.

"Do you want to talk to her?"

"No." But her voice was small.

"Well, I'm curious now, so if you won't talk to her maybe I will."

Elan didn't want to admit it, but she was curious. What could Jess possibly have to say? Elan wanted to know, but she also didn't. Deep inside she was hopeful, but she knew from the many let-downs life had dealt her that hope didn't stand a chance. Mentally she started wrapping layers of protection around her heart.

Todd drummed his fingers on the counter. "Well?"

"I don't know." She felt suddenly lost.

"Look Elan," he said, "Let me give you some advice from an idiot who made the wrong choice once…talk to her. If you don't, it will eat at you and eat at you until all you have are the doubts, the fears and the 'what ifs' circling like vultures, pecking at you and eating at your life. It is better to know the truth than to spend days, months, and possibly even years wondering what would or even could have been—if you would have just talked to her."

She scowled at him. "Fine." She untied her apron. "Tell Eli I am taking a break."

"I already talked to him. He said it was okay as long as you stopped at the market and picked up some fresh veggies. I have a list and his card." He handed her a scrap of scribbled on paper and the Secrets Café credit card.

Elan took them and shoved them in her back pocket. This was why she liked Todd. He understood. He was there for her. It was what made him a good friend and someone to rely on. "Thank you Todd." She put her coat on and the red scarf she had found.

"We'll see how you feel about that later." He gave her a shove. "And don't forget the groceries!"

Elan stepped out of the kitchen and into the main room. She scanned the area and saw Jess sitting at the bar, stirring a to go cup of coffee. She was happy to see Jess looked like she had been crying. Good, Elan wanted her to be hurt. She walked over to Jess, and they stared into each other's eyes, saying nothing but speaking everything.

Elan broke the silence. "I need to go to Pikes for some supplies." She held out the list, "Let's go for a walk."

Jess picked up her coffee and followed her outside.

Shades of gray clouds moved across the pale blue sky, lingering, waiting, threatening rain. Leaves drifted like tears falling from the trees as they walked away from Secrets, down Union Street towards Pikes Place Market. It was a perfect fall day, beautiful yet sad with autumn's cries. Elan put her hands in her pockets and kept her head down. They traipsed wordlessly through the crowds.

"Look, I'm sorry," Jess finally said as they reached

the corner of Union and First Avenue.

"How long have you been sleeping with her?" Elan didn't believe in dancing around the subject. She stopped walking and looked at Jess.

"Sleeping with her?"

"I think I deserve to know."

"Is that what she told you?" Jess pushed the button on the streetlamp to cross. "Look, you know Shayla and I have been friends for a long time."

"Yeah. So?"

Jess rubbed her forehead. "Shayla is messed up. She had a hard childhood and lived a very sheltered life—"

"Spare me the psychobabble analysis."

"Fine. Fine." Jess finished her coffee, tossed the empty cup into a nearby trash bin, and stood in front of Elan. "She made this shit up. I slept with her once before I met you. *Once*. She called you this morning because she's scared I will leave her. She likes to play these fucked up games with people."

"Honest?" Elan wanted to believe her.

Jess gently touched Elan's face. "I told her I was falling in love with you and she got all upset. Turns out she has been seeing this other woman, someone older, and Shayla broke it off with her a month ago because Shayla was supposedly developing feelings for me. So she said. She was desperate. When I told her about you, about how I felt, she came unglued and cried, threw one of her tantrums. She took a knife to her wrist and threatened to kill herself. She does this shit off and on. The only way I could get her to stop was to tell her I was through with you. I woke up when she was talking to you. I tried to call you."

"I know." Elan looked away, blinking back tears.

She pushed her hands deep into her pockets.

They crossed the street to the market. Jess continued, "I never meant to hurt you. I didn't think she would call you. I thought she would play her stupid knife game and then it would blow over. When I heard her on the phone, I lost it. I told her I was through with her, that I loved you, and I wanted to be with you and that…that I no longer wanted to live with her."

"So, you weren't girlfriends?" Elan didn't dare breathe.

"No, just friends."

They stopped next to one of the flower stalls. Elan looked at the rows of dried flowers all wrapped in bundles of vibrant colors, and thought about how just this morning she had wanted Jess to move in with her. Her morning had been a roller coaster of emotions, dreams, fantasies, and the phone call. Could she trust Jess?

"I told her to get out," Jess said.

"You did?" Elan's voice was broken, afraid.

"Yes. I told her I love you."

"You did?"

Jess smiled at the repetitive statement. "Yes, Elan, I did."

Elan thought about that. It was good. Yet scary. She fingered one of the bouquets. "This morning, before the call, I dreamed about what it would be like to live with you. I was thinking about how we could go shopping together at Pikes, pick out fruit and vegetables for dinner, maybe some flowers for the table."

"Flowers?"

"I don't know what your favorite flowers are." Elan sighed. "Look, I know we haven't been going out for that long and we haven't done any of the overnight stuff and

I know I have issues and you have your bat-shit crazy roommate." Jess gave a nervous laugh at that. "I just…this morning…" Elan broke off.

Jess glanced down the aisle at all of the different bouquets. "My favorite flowers are Dahlias." She reached past Elan for a bouquet with a rich red dahlia surrounded by yellow and orange mums. "I would have bought this bunch because they remind me of your fire and your vibrancy."

Elan didn't know what to say to that. She looked away and bit at her lip. A tear formed at the edge of her eye, and she wiped it clear. "I need to get some stuff for the bar." She took the list out and walked past the flowers to the vegetable stalls.

"Stop Elan." Jess reached out and took her hand. "You said you wondered what it would be like to shop for food at Pikes together." They faced each other as people wove past them, with the fish mongers voices crying out their wares. Jess took the list from Elan. "Now, what do we need?"

The walls Elan had built trembled, rattled, and started to crumble. Yet she still was unsure. Her fears made her hesitate.

"Let's see…" Jess scanned the list. "Carrots, celery, radishes, grapes, red peppers, cauliflower, broccoli, and honey. What is he making?"

"Most of it's for salad. The broccoli and cauliflower we sauté in olive oil with some garlic pepper. So, so good." Elan perused the stalls picking up assorted items from the list.

"Okay, we can do this. It's not too long," Jess said and passed Elan a couple of red peppers.

The shopping eased the doubts back and helped Elan

relax. When Jess accidentally sprinkled Elan with water from a bundle of celery, she laughed. She couldn't help herself. It felt natural. They wandered the aisles selecting the right items, comparing them to others before purchasing them. Elan's anger from earlier slipped its grip and retreated. She watched as Jess sampled one of the honeys, her mouth open, tongue flicking out to catch a tiny drip.

"Try this one." Jess held out a little spoon from a spicy honey batch.

Elan tasted it, the flavor sweet at first before the spice kicked in. "Wow."

"I know right?" Jess gave her the kind of smile that could light a room, bring a city to its knees with its brightness, its warmth. Elan pulled Jess close, kissing her. It was soft, like Elan was walking on ice and unsure of her footing, but then it became hungry, more urgent and Elan forgot all about her hurt heart. She forgot all about being in the middle of Pikes and let herself melt into Jess, who felt like home and tasted like honey and cinnamon.

"Forgive me?" Jess whispered when they broke apart.

"Yes."

"I was so mad at her this morning." Jess bit the edge of her lip.

"Then why didn't you grab the phone from her?"

"I did, but you'd hung up." Jess let her hair fall like a curtain in front of her face. "I grabbed the phone from her and when she laughed, I hit her. I slapped her Elan. I have never hit anyone in my life, and I wished I could have done more. I screamed at her to get out. I told her we were through and when she grabbed the knife again,

I told her to use it this time and stop faking. I went in my room and called you. When you didn't answer again and again I called Secrets and asked Todd if you were in."

"Todd…"

"He told me you were there. I wanted to talk to you in person, face to face."

"So, it was a lie."

"Everything she told you was a crock of shit," Jess said, "When I came out of my room, she was gone. So I left. I had to see you, to tell you in person and, most importantly, I needed to tell you I love you."

"Good, because I love you too." Elan kissed her again. A couple people passing by clapped. Someone said, "Get a room!" Someone else whistled. Elan broke it off with a giggle. A street vendor started playing a love song.

"Oh my God," Elan put a hand to her face, blushing.

"Wow." Jess buried her head in Elan's shoulder.

"So, what do we do about your roommate?"

"Nothing. I'm done with her. I stood by her for so long and let her use me, I can't do it anymore. She's draining. There's only so much I can take. I'm through with her games." Jess traced Elan's chin line. "I'm tired of putting my life on hold for her. I want you. I want to see where we are going, what is in store for us, and if that means letting the noose of Shayla and I's friendship fall to the wayside then so be it. It is long overdue. Trust me."

"Trust you." Could she do that? Elan wanted to trust her.

Jess raised earnest eyes to her. "Please."

Elan bit her lip, thinking. "You weren't the liar," she finally said. "Shayla was. And she can fuck off. I'm sorry I believed her and didn't give you a chance to explain."

"She's good at what she does."

"And what's that?"

"Playing games. Manipulating people's lives." Jess leaned back in Elan's arms, toying with the edge of the scarf she had on. "Where did you get this scarf?"

"Work. It was left on a table." Elan didn't care about the scarf. "Why?"

"It looks familiar…but whatever." Jess bit at her lip. "So, what now?"

"Now? I think you need to walk me back to work."

"I can do that." Jess grabbed Elan's hand.

Elan brought her hand to her lips and kissed it. "I don't want to be apart from you."

"Me either. Just the thought of losing you hurt."

"I felt the same way." They walked towards Secrets Café, stopping at the light. Elan kissed her again. Jess's lips were soft, sweet, and Elan didn't want to stop. The light changed, the people around them began to move and they broke apart.

Jess gripped both of Elan's hands. "I don't want to go back to my place."

"Are you scared?"

"A bit. I don't think she would hurt me, but I don't want to be anywhere around her."

"You could stay at my place." Elan had a small apartment with one bedroom, a tiny living area, and a kitchen which consisted of just a fridge, sink, and small stove. Jess had been there many times.

"That would be nice…" Jess looked down at the ground. "Just for tonight?"

"No." Elan drew in her courage. "Move in with me." The words once spoken broke down her walls of fear. She wanted to wake up to Jess, to fall asleep with her, and to come home to her arms. She wanted Jess, now and forever she wanted Jess.

"Are you sure?"

"Yes." She stepped over her crumbled fear and took Jess in her arms, crushing her body tight, and knew in her heart they belonged together. She kissed Jess and felt the blood rush between them, felt the hunger and need rise. Time was lost, sound ceased to exist: it was just a longing between them. Jess undid the buttons of Elan's jacket and ran her hand under her shirt, sending shivers across Elan's skin. Jess unknotted the scarf so she could have better access to Elan's neck. The scarf fluttered loose, falling like a serpent upon the ground: neither of them noticed or cared. When the kiss broke off they were both breathing hard.

"I have to get back to work." Elan groaned.

"We're almost there."

They started walking again. "I wish I didn't have to go."

"It's okay, honest." Jess squeezed her hand. "Thank you for forgiving me."

"Thank you for making me listen."

They rounded the corner to Secrets Café. Elan led Jess down the alley to the back entry. Pushing the door open, Elan held a finger to her lips to shush Jess, and they tiptoed into the kitchen. Elan set the bag of groceries down, made sure it was clear before taking Jess into the bathroom, bolting the door and pushing her against the stall.

"Tell me again, how you feel?" Elan whispered in Jess's ear, opening her jacket, and pushing her shirt up so Elan's lips could find the hard little nipples hidden by Jess's bra.

Jess arched her back, and gasped. "I love you."

"Shh, I love you too. Now quiet."

"Oh, that will be challenging," Jess whispered as Elan unzipped Jess's jeans, slipped her hand under the panties, traced the silken wetness between Jess's legs and inserted a finger. It was warm inside, like molten heat Elan could stroke and build to a fire.

"Oh shit." Jess wrapped her arms around Elan and held on.

"Shh baby." Elan rocked her hand back and forth, keeping the one finger inside, adding pressure to the clit with her thumb. She scissored her fingers alongside the lips of the vulva, increasing her strokes. Jess pushed her hips forward to get more and bit back a cry. Elan's fingers slipped in the wetness, losing the clit. She repositioned them.

"Oh God…yes…"

Elan settled into a rhythm, listening to the moans from Jess, feeling the heat from her pussy. Keeping the pressure on Jess's clit, Elan intensified her strokes, feeling the smooth velvet of Jess's skin, the heat and fire of her inner core.

Jess started to gasp out, "Right there…don't stop…"

"Elan." It was Todd at the door, he kept his voice low. "Eli is looking for you."

"Shit." Elan jumped. For a moment she had forgotten where she was. She leaned back and covered her mouth, stifling a giggle. Jess stood frozen, her orgasm lost.

"I'll be out in a minute."

"Hurry," Todd added.

Elan removed her hand from Jess's pants. "I'm sorry." She whispered, shaking her head.

"It's okay." Jess giggled and zipped her pants up.

Elan helped Jess get her shirt down, tangling it in her bra and laughed which started Jess laughing as well.

Jess straightened her jacket, flipped her hair back, smiled into Elan's eyes and whispered, "We can try again tonight."

"Tonight," Elan repeated the word, tasting it, savoring it.

"Yes. It's okay that I get some of my stuff and take it to your place, right?"

"Of course, yeah." Elan reached into her pocket and handed over the keys. Jess closed her hand over Elan's, the keys clasped between them. They stared into each other's eyes. Elan felt a door inside open to possibilities, to a future she was still a bit scared of wandering into but wanted to explore.

"Elan?" It was Todd again.

"You better get back to work." Jess half-heartedly pushed her.

"I know." Elan kissed her.

"And tonight, you can help me settle in."

"Wait, Todd's band plays tonight. I promised Eli I would stay till eight to help set things up."

"Todd's band?" Jess furrowed her brow.

"It's the play offs." Elan explained, "The battle of the bands."

"Oh! Yeah, there was a sign on the door."

"Will you come with me tonight?"

"I'm down for that."

"Elan," Todd hissed through the door again.

"I know, I know. I'm coming."

"We don't have time for that," He replied, cracking Elan and Jess up so they had to cover their mouths to stifle the giggles.

"I'll go out the back." Jess pushed Elan away from her. "You get back to work, I need to go get my stuff. We need to be responsible right now."

"You're right. You're right." Elan closed her eyes and drew in a breath. She opened the door, turned back to Jess, and whispered, "I love you."

"I love you too. Now go."

Elan walked out on cloud nine.

Todd was waiting around the corner. He arched an eyebrow at her and tugged at his beard. "I take it things went well?"

"Very." She gave him a Cheshire cat grin.

He shoved her playfully. "Well, are you going to tell me? Come on."

"You want to know?" She shoved him back as they stepped into the kitchen.

"Yes."

"We are in love." She sang it out.

"Oh lord." Todd rolled his eyes. "What did she say about everything? What happened? Was it true? Did she beg for forgiveness?"

"It's a secret," Elan replied and wiggled her eyebrows. She picked up one of the two salad bowls he had prepped for her and carried it out the door. Todd followed with some salad plates.

Todd shook his head. "I can't believe you're not going to tell me."

Elan grinned. "I will give you this much. The roommate was a freakin' liar, we figured everything out and Jess is moving in with me." She looked towards the large window fronting the Café and watched as Jess strolled past, waving at Elan before she was gone, like a leaf blowing in the breeze. "It's a new beginning."

The door opened and the first of the afternoon regulars started to spill in. To her, it felt like a year had passed in the space of an hour. So much had happened. Her whole world had been flipped over from where it started in the morning. She was a new person, reborn, someone on the verge of something magical, and all the heartache and tears she had endured didn't matter. They were just a fleeting thought, a momentary slip backwards. Everything was back in order now and Elan needed to get through the rest of the day until she could see Jess again.

She walked up to the first table, smiled at the attractive blonde and said, "Welcome to Secrets."

Secret Rant

She left me for her? Seriously? The girl looks like a boy! She has a shaved head! And she's nothing but a fucking waitress! Seriously...what the hell? I could kill her! I could kill the stupid waitress! What the hell is the bitch's name? It was on her name tag, something weird, foreign sounding, not Ellen but like that multi-millionaire...whatever. Bitch is going down. I'll ruin her and that's a promise.

Chapter 5

Secret Hook Up

Sometimes it was as simple as eyes meeting eyes across the way and a knowing look of mutual desire. This could be done quickly, one glance, one up and down sweep followed by a smile of invitation. If the attraction was mutual the bait would be taken, and she would be followed to her destination where after a brief conversation Nina could decide if the prey was worthy of more.

Nina Monroe was on her way to get lunch at Secrets Café when she paused at the light and caught the eye of a handsome, swarthy looking man on the opposite side of the street. She lowered her glasses and their eyes locked, dark brown on blue steel and she took her time checking him out. He was well built, nice hair, with a certain cockiness in his stance. He smiled and licked his lips.

The light changed and she glanced over at her prey to make sure he was watching, gave him a half smile and strode purposefully past him, her hips a come follow me invitation. She dodged around a young lesbian couple oblivious to the crowd, their arms wrapped around each other, lips locked, a red scarf coming undone and fluttering to their feet. Nina felt his eyes zero in on her and straightened her spine, shoulders back, chest high, like a peacock flaring its tail.

Nina opened the door to Secrets Café and narrowly missed running into a woman with out-of-control red hair carrying a notebook. The side stepped each other, the woman passed and Nina stepped inside, letting her eyes adjust before finding a private table near the back. Unbuttoning her coat, she draped it over her chair and surveyed the area. She preferred places more upscale compared to Secrets Café but it had a certain pull to it, a certain edge the darker more secretive part of her liked. She crossed her sculpted legs and picked up a menu with her manicured hands. Flipping a strand of her chin length blonde hair out of her view, Nina watched the door. Had she been wrong? Had she misread the signals? She waited.

"Hi, welcome to Secrets." A skinny young woman with a name badge identifying her as Elan flipped her order pad open and smiled down at Nina. "May I get you a drink?"

"Water please," she replied. "With lemon."

Elan walked away and there he was, standing in the doorway dressed in molded denim with a tight black button-down shirt, under a sweat jacket. He was carrying a red scarf. He had taken the bait, now, to see if he was worth it.

Nina raised her chin, met his eyes, and gave him the briefest nod. Her gray blue eyes appraised him as he moved towards her, striding like a panther approaching prey, and she felt her pulse quicken. He was lean, muscular. She wondered what he looked like without his clothes on.

He regarded her from deep brown eyes, pulled out the chair next to her, and sat down. "I think you dropped this." He held out the scarf.

She took it. It wasn't hers, but it was expensive. "Thank you."

He held out his hand. "I'm Carlos." His voice was whiskey soft with a hint of danger and she knew she was in trouble.

"Nina." She took his hand; It was surprisingly smooth and firm. He held onto hers running his fingers across her skin.

"I hope you don't mind if I join you," he whispered and licked his lips.

"I don't mind at all." She ran a finger along her chin line.

They eyed each other and she felt the temperature rise between them, a steady slow burning pulse of desire. She could feel his eyes rove over her, from her breasts, the curve of her waist, her hips to her naked legs, and back to her lips. He scooted his chair closer. She bit her lip. He was still holding her hand.

"You are very beautiful," he whispered. "I noticed that as you walked past me. You made my heart race in such a way that I had to follow you." His fingers traveled lightly from her wrist to her forearm and up her shoulder; She felt fire trails break out on her skin under her clothes. God he was intoxicating. She wished she was naked.

"Thank you," she replied.

He reached out and cupped her chin, letting his fingers graze along her jawline and she closed her eyes, feeling the heat from him.

"So…so beautiful," he whispered.

"Thank you," she repeated and opened her eyes. She was hungry but not for food.

Two glasses of water were set on the table with a

small plate of sliced lemon. "I took the liberty of bringing a second glass." Elan beamed. "Are we ready to order?"

Nina recomposed herself and replied, "The house salad." Food didn't sound really good, but she had a brief to put together and needed some sort of sustenance other than what the delicious man next to her was subtly offering.

"And for you sir?" Elan turned to the man.

"The steak salad. And a coke please."

"I'll be right back." Elan smiled at them both before leaving.

"So," Nina smoothed her skirt, "Carlos, do you work near here?"

"Not too far."

"What do you do?" She asked.

"I don't think what I do for a living matters right now…" he replied and scooted his chair a hair closer.

Nina smiled and licked her lips. "And what do you think does matter?"

"I think what matters, is what I can do for *you*."

This, she liked. He was perfect. He may not have matched anything on her list, but he would be a perfect fuckable treat. Like an appetizer. Nina inclined her head towards his and let her gaze traverse his face. "You think you know what I like?"

"I think I could satisfy your needs."

She laughed at the boldness of him and took a sip of water. "How old are you?"

"Thirty-three," he took her hand again, "Does age matter?"

She gave a low laugh. "Just wanted to be sure you were over twenty-one."

"How old are you?"

"Old enough to know better," she replied and withdrew her hand.

"But young enough to do it anyway?" He placed his hand dangerously close to the edge of her skirt.

She looked down at his fingers: they were long, smooth and she could feel the heat of his touch. She looked up into his eyes and he was watching her, waiting. She shifted in her chair and parted her legs, wondering if he would take the bait or if he was all talk.

"Yes." She dared him.

Elan returned with their salads and set them down.

"I don't know if I can eat." Nina glanced down at her salad.

"You're going to need your strength." Carlos kept his hand on her thigh and traced the skin just under her skirt.

"You're quite sure of yourself, aren't you?" She placed her free hand on his hip and inched it towards the growing bulge in his pants. He pushed it onto his hardening cock.

"Yes, I am."

Nina blushed and gave a low laugh. "Oh Lord."

He grinned. "No, Carlos."

She shook her head, smiling at the cheekiness of it, the boldness, and took a bite of her salad doing her best to get her heart to stop racing. He was turning her on, making her wet. She shifted in her chair.

"So…Carlos, tell me about yourself. Are you from here?"

"Arizona," he replied, "But this is boring talk. Why don't I tell you what I would like to do to you instead? That is far more exciting than all the rest."

"Are you…" She searched for the right word, leaned in close, and whispered in his ear, "Safe?"

"As in," He whispered back, "Sexually?"

His breath was hot on her neck. "Yes." She turned to face him. Their lips were scant inches apart.

"I'm safe." He looked down at her lips, moved in closer.

Nina waited, ready for a kiss but he backed off. "I don't know about that," she said, arching an eyebrow at him.

He laughed and slipped his hand between her legs, letting his fingers stop just outside the entrance to her pussy, feeling her heat, her desire. "Here is what I know," he whispered in her ear. His breath was a hot invitation.

Control, she told herself, maintain control. She didn't move, she didn't want to give her desire away.

"I know you want to feel me inside you." He pushed her panties aside and let a finger run up and down her vulva.

She gasped and glanced around the café, hoping no one could see. Once she was convinced no was watching she spread her legs further. He slid a finger in and placed his thumb on her eager for action clit.

"Tell me you don't want me." He dipped a fork into his salad while gently stroking her with his finger.

"I can't," she whispered back. She was amazed at how calm he was. She was amazed at his brazen touch. She was amazed he had her so turned on and his fingers were inside her and she wanted to cry out, to let herself go but there were too many people, and he was just sitting there, one hand teasing her while casually eating.

"Here," He plucked a small cherry tomato from her

plate, "Open your mouth."

She did as he asked and he slipped the tomato between her lips. She let her mouth close on his fingers licking him before he pulled them out. The sensation of his fingers in her mouth, feeding her, and his fingers inside her pussy were magic. She bit into the tomato, tasting the sweet juice and watched as he picked up another one.

She ate that one as well.

"I like watching your mouth." He grinned.

She wanted more of him. "You should see what else I can do with it." Her voice was a husky seduction. She rubbed at the bulge in his pants. Deliberately, slowly, she dug into her lunch and ate a forkful.

"You are very wet," he whispered.

"You are very hard." She could play this game.

He scooted even closer to her until they were bare inches away. She draped one knee over his legs giving him better access to her but keeping their actions hidden from the patrons. She faced him and glanced from his eyes to his lips, to his eyes, to his lips. She paused just a moment before giving in and kissing him. He kept his finger inside her working it in and out. She felt the hunger in her build, her desire swell, grow and she reached for him, devouring his lips, bruising his mouth until she forgot where she was and gave in, yielding to his strokes, to his insistent kisses.

He broke off and she stared at him with lust filled eyes, heart pounding, trying to catch her breath He was what she wanted right now. They were from different worlds, different cultures, different stations in life…but it was just sex, right? And sex was what she needed.

"I have an hour until I have to be back at work." Her

panties were soaked.

"I need two." He raised an eyebrow. "Call them and tell them you are running late."

"Where will we go?" She was thinking out loud. She wasn't about to take him back to her place. Didn't know him that well, wasn't sure if she wanted to know him beyond a good fuck, knowing her place wasn't an option.

"I have an apartment just down the street." He suggested, sipping his soda.

She could just imagine it, some place small and dirty, with five roommates. There had to be something better. Oh yes! The office kept a hotel room available at The Executive on Spring Street. It was a short walk away.

"I have a better place in mind." She pulled out her phone.

He took his fingers out of her wet pussy and licked them. "You taste delicious."

"Oh my God," Nina shook her head. "I want you to know—I just want to be clear, I'm not looking for anything other than sex."

"Works for me." He shrugged and ate another mouthful of salad.

"How do I know I can trust you and you aren't after anything else?" She wanted to be sure. He wasn't the first man she'd picked up for a moment of passion, but one never knew if a good time was going to turn in to a bad mistake or worse.

Carlos laughed, reached in his pocket, took out his wallet, and handed it to her. "My driver's license is in here...write everything down Nina. I'm not after anything but your pleasure."

She hesitated, weighing the pros and cons. It was a

dangerous world out there; All sorts of things could happen. She could end up being raped, murdered, on the five o-clock news, mugged, robbed, beaten…or…he could just ravish her, fuck her, and please her. She liked the last idea the best. She was in desperate need of a good fuck.

He watched her as she debated. "Think about this," he waved a hand about the café, "This place is full. The waitress knows what we ordered and what we had to drink. She can describe both of us to the officials if need be."

He had a point. Nina glanced around again. She saw the waitress talking to the brown-haired barista, and the skinny young blonde girl with the glasses who was cleaning tables. They would remember her leaving with the hot young Latino. Who wouldn't? He was hard not to notice. She and Carlos would need to leave separately, and if they ended up hooking up again, Secrets Café would make a great spot for an in between. She took out her phone, stared into his eyes, and dialed the receptionist at the firm.

"Kellie, Nina here." She listened. "Yes, I know. Look I have to run home, I forgot some paperwork." She listened some more. "Yes, well, it can't be helped. Tell Lowan I have an affair to attend to and I will contact him when I return." She nodded while Kellie said something. "No, it's nothing to do with that. Promise." Whatever Kellie said made her laugh, "I promise, next time okay. This time is strictly business. Will you hold my calls. Thank you." She hung up, dialed another number, "Hi, this is Nina from Jones and Forester. I have a client I am bringing over for some briefing." She listened, nodded. "Thank you, we will be there shortly." She slipped her phone back in her purse, took a sip of water and turned her smoldering eyes to his. "You know where The Executive Hotel is?"

He nodded. "Spring Street."

"Meet me there." She stood up, dusted any possible crumbs off her red skirt, and adjusted her grey silk top, before pulling on her long white coat. She gave her hair a careful toss and set a twenty on the table. He leaned back and watched her, like a cat watching a mouse. Well, she would show him just who the cat was.

"You want me to wait while you leave?" He clarified.

"Yes. No."

"Which is it?" he raised an eyebrow.

Nina hesitated, there was no reason why they couldn't leave together. No one knew them. But then again, what if she ran into someone she knew on the way to the Hotel? Separate would be better, just for appearances sake.

"Separate," she replied, nodding her head. It was just sex. Hopefully it would be as promising as he looked. She liked a man with stamina, a man who could play, and a man she could keep as a secret. He certainly didn't match the man on her list for the future, but he matched the craving she had for something strange.

She didn't wait to see if he was following. Instinct told her he was. She strode out the door, high heels clicking on the pavement and walked to the hotel feeling his eyes trace her body.

Picking up the key at the front desk of the hotel, she waited at the elevator until he joined her, standing apart until the doors slid shut.

Chapter 6

Midnight Secrets

At night Secrets Cafe transformed into a bar that catered to the neighborhood. Thursday through Saturday night, live bands competed. There were generally two playing a night. The crowd would vote on them, and the winner would advance into the finals held in June or December in what was known as the Final Countdown. The winner of that competition was chosen to play on either the Fourth of July or New Year's Eve and offered a recording contract.

Todd and his band Monkeys Breath were playing tonight. He had been nervous for most of the day but now that it was here, he drew in a deep breath, and stepped out onto the stage. He stared into the too bright, and hotter than anyone realized, lights and waited for the lead chords to begin. Monkeys Breath started with a rocking tune, the crowd cheered, and Todd began to relax.

When the chords of the third song strummed in, the one he had written, he was in the zone. He waited for the drum break, drew in a breath, let it out, and started to sing:

If I have one regret
It's that I didn't let you know
How I stood at the window
And just watched you go

How I listened to pride
Instead of my heart
How I knew it was wrong
Right from the start
How I didn't run after you
And beg you to stay
And now I must live with that
For the rest of my days…

He forgot the crowd, forgot the cheers, and tuned the noise out. He was one with the notes, the chords, and the vibration of the strings. Before he even realized it, their hour and a half set was done. Todd stood with the sweat dripping down his back and listened to the roar of the crowd bringing him back to earth. It was a high he would choose over and over and over again if he could. He stepped off the stage with the rest of his crew, out of the bright lights, and into reality.

"That was great!" Someone said. Faces were still a blur to him.

"Holy shit Todd!" Elan smacked him on the back. He recognized her voice. "You did great!"

"Thank you. Thank you." He smiled at her and wiped his forehead with his sleeve. He needed to clean up. "Thanks for coming."

"Whatever." She laughed, "Go put your stuff away and meet me up front. We'll buy you a drink."

"Sounds good." He needed a drink, something cold with lots of ice. He carried his guitar into the back room, tucked it safely into its case and listened as the next band started to set up. The crowd was huge tonight. He hoped they got a good score. His friend Jason came in with his bass and put it away as well.

"Great job out there!" Ash, their drummer, clapped

him on the back.

"You too," he replied, "How do you think we did?"

"Good. I don't want to jinx anything, but I think we nailed it."

Todd crossed his fingers and raised them. Taking his shirt off, he wiped his face down and changed into the extra T-shirt he'd brought. He ran his hands through his thick tangle of brown hair and pulled it back into a tail. He tugged at a few long strands in his clipped beard, knowing he'd missed a few. They drove him crazy. It was a nervous habit to check them repeatedly.

"Ladies and Gentlemen," Eli Jones, the owner of the café who was doubling as the announcer, did his best to calm the crowd down. "Quiet everyone, quiet." More cheers and whistles. Todd laughed, wet his hair line down, and stepped out into the thick of it. "Thank you for coming. I'd like to thank Monkeys Breath for their great performance and now I am happy to bring to the stage the musical tunes of Void."

The crowd erupted in more cheers and Todd made his way to the line at the bar. The vibe was high. People stopped him on the way, clapping him on the back and singing praises. He was humbled and grateful. He caught Elan's eye and waved. She was standing with Jess, clearly their little liaison earlier had resulted in a make-up of proportional results. It was written all over the way they were hanging onto each other. He was glad. Elan deserved some happiness.

"Hey ladies!" He shouted over the crowd.

"You were great!" Jess cupped her hands to her mouth and shouted back.

"Thanks!"

Elan caught Jay's eye and motioned for a drink. Elan

then pointed to Todd. Jay gave Todd a nod and held up a bottle of rum. He gave Jay the okay.

"You played really well." A long dark-haired woman beamed up at him.

"Thank you." She looked vaguely familiar, but he wasn't sure from where. She held out her hand and he shook it. She smiled at him, gave him a slow look over, and walked away. For a moment Todd stood there. Hypnotized. Elan shouted to him, and he snapped out of the trance, hurrying to her.

"Hey guys." He gave them a hug.

Jess had snagged a couple of seats at the bar. She motioned for him to sit down but he was too wired. Elan handed him his glass. Todd took a long drink, feeling the liquid cool the heat of his racing heart. His hands were shaking from the adrenaline still pumping through him. He set the drink down on the counter. The woman next to them looked over.

"Good job up there." She pushed her glasses back.

"Thanks," he replied. She turned back to her notebook. He recognized her. She was a regular. The mystery woman: liked to come in for coffee in the mornings, she worked nearby. Her name was on the tip of his tongue but his brain was still reeling from his performance. He needed another drink.

"I think you'll win." Elan was ever his supporter, his sister from another mother.

"I hope so. Void is pretty good though." He watched as the next band finished plugging everything in and started to check their sound system. He needed them to suck. At the same time, he didn't want to invoke Karma by wishing they would suck. He just wanted Void to not play as well as Monkeys Breath had.

The music from the jukebox faded, the lights dimmed. The lead singer adjusted a few things, hit a chord, let it reverberate around the room, circle, and swoop. He strummed another and nodded to the bass guitarist who joined in.

"Here we go." Todd readied himself. This was it.

Void started playing, of all things, a ballad:

It begins sometime after midnight…

It was about forgetting yourself and being lost. Todd didn't think it was a good choice to keep the crowd riled. The song was haunting, a bit hypnotic, filled with regret and carried a good beat. He was analyzing it, studying the reaction of the crowd, when he saw her. Jennie.

His whole world collapsed. Everything slowed down. It was like being in a movie with time frozen and no one moving except for her. Jennie. She was laughing. She was smiling that smile that turned the world on fire. She was wearing the white dress that always made him think of summer. Her hair was a bit longer but still honey colored with mixed hues of gold and darker brown. His heart stopped. His world stopped and he was suddenly struck back in time to the first moment he ever saw her leaning against the wall at the college opener dance two years ago, wearing jeans and a flowy cotton tank top.

****

She was alone, trying hard to appear confident and look like she belonged, but he sensed she was unsure. Walking up to her, Todd introduced himself, and asked if she would like to dance. She turned him down. "I need to get to know you first before I let you get that close to me."

"Well then, how about we sit and talk for a bit." He led her over to a table where they started comparing high school stories, growing up stories, likes and dislikes. They laughed and shared, and just before the last song was about to play, she reached out, put her hand on his arm and said, "Okay Todd, let's dance."

Her touch sent electric shocks through his body. He took her arm and guided her to the floor, into the middle of the crowd and she twirled into his arms. Just having her that close was enough to make his heart race. She reached up, put her hand on his chest and gazed into his eyes.

"I can feel your heartbeat," she whispered.

He held her close, pressed her lithe body against his. "I can feel yours as well."

They stared at each other gently swaying to the music and kissed the kind of kiss that melted everything away and left him wanting more.

****

"Todd?" Elan prodded him with an elbow.

He came back to reality and drew his eyes away from Jennie, the one who got away, the one who broke his heart, the one—if he was completely honest with himself—that he'd hurt.

"Sorry." He shook his head, trying to come back to the present.

"You okay?" She asked. "You look like you've seen a ghost or something."

He drew a long swallow of his drink, and his eyes went back to Jennie in that white dress, standing in the crowd.

Elan followed his gaze. "Shit. Is that…?"

He nodded and just as he was about to say her name, Jennie turned and saw him. For a moment there was a hesitation on her part. It made him wonder how long she had been there. Had she heard him play? Had she known he was going to be there tonight? The questions swirled in his head like a strange cocktail mixing the past with the present. He didn't know what to do, but when she smiled at him, he was lost all over again. Downing his drink, Todd handed the empty glass to Elan. She knew him well and ordered another.

Jennie walked through the crowd, parting the waves like Moses, and stood before him. She looked the same. She looked like time had not touched her, like he could literally fall back into what had once been, change the past, and still be with her.

"I saw your set-"

He said at the same time, "—I didn't know you were back in town."

They stopped and tried again.

****

The memories crashed into him like waves on a shore and he could see her the first time they made love, see the way moonlight spilled a tattoo across her back as he undressed her, slowly, like a gift he'd been waiting forever to open. He unveiled her skin, her body, her perfect curves, and she trembled as she stood before him.

"What do I do?" He asked suddenly unsure, tugging at his beard, wanting the moment to be perfect and scared he might mess it up.

"Touch me, slip your fingers inside." She whispered, nibbling his ear, "Use your thumb to rub the clit. Get me wet and…" she gave out a soft moan as he followed her directions. "Yes, yes, that's it. Oh you are good. You sure you haven't done this before?" Her voice was like honey.

He had, but not with someone he really cared about,

someone he wanted to get off. "Not like this." He kissed her, feeling her body respond and open to him. "Let me taste you." He begged breaking away.

"Please." Her voice was a breathless sigh as he trailed kisses down her neck, her chest and knelt before her. He slipped his tongue into the wetness of her, felt her fingers clutch at his hair, heard her cry out as he drew in the heady scent of her. Jennie.

He remembered fumbling with the rubber, not getting it right, and how she reached over and slipped it on while whispering about practicing at school on a banana. She kissed him, stroked him, and held his hardening cock in her hands before guiding it between her legs into her warmth.

She was his second. He was her third. They made love for hours.

****

The noise of Secrets Café brought him into the present. Jennie was really there, standing before him, and he could smell her perfume. It was the same scent he'd been searching for, the one that lingered every now and then in the air. It was the one that reminded him of spring when the sun came out, calling forth the flowers and the trees and grass shining with life. She was looking at him the way she had before when she would listen to him play his guitar and watch him like a cat. He remembered how he would ask her what she was thinking, and she would reply, "I want to know if you can play me like that."

He would put his guitar down, take her in his arms, bury his face in the scent of her and play her like the instrument she was. He would draw out her moans, her sighs, and strum her with his fingers, his lips, his tongue, and, finally, his cock.

God, he loved her scent. He closed his eyes and tried to stay in the present.

"You still wear that perfume." It wasn't a question.

"Yes," she replied, "It has always been my favorite."

They were silent, two lovers now strangers separated by a gulf of time and unspoken words that lingered and waited, wondering if they would be spoken.

He knew there were things he should say, words he needed to speak but he was unable to formulate anything except the simple thought of Jennie. Jennie was here.

"I've missed you." It was out before he could stop the words. He had no business saying them. The problem was…they were true.

Jennie lowered her head and bit at her lip, and he remembered kissing her, tasting her, curling up naked next to her in the moonlight on their bed, holding her, breathing her in. She looked up at him and he was too late. He had fucked it up long ago and there was no going back. Her eyes spoke volumes.

She reached up, brushed a hand along his chin line. "It's good to see you again Todd."

"You too." He wanted to say more but couldn't.

She waited just a moment, turned, and was gone, swallowed up in the crowd, a ghost he could never have again. He reached out for the bar and caught hold of it. His legs felt weak.

Elan was immediately there. She started to order for him. He stopped her, he needed something stronger.

"Whiskey," he said, "A double."

Jay quickly poured him a drink. He took it, clutching the glass tight as if it was the only thing he could feel. His heart pounded in his chest, wanting to go back in time, knowing it was too late, knowing he could never get her back that she was gone—*gone* gone. He was a fool, an idiot and the memory of their breakup crashed into him like thunder, like lightning, like a hurricane.

****

They had been together for nine months and living together for six. Jennie was in the kitchen, cooking macaroni and cheese for dinner. He was in the main area of their studio practicing his guitar.

Normally she liked to listen to him but this time she was on her phone ignoring him. They had argued a few days earlier. He'd found a text from one of her study partners, someone named Daniel, asking if she could meet him later and she responded she couldn't talk to him and here they were two days later. Todd accused her of cheating on him. She denied it of course and pointed out the time she caught him hanging all over Brooke at the gym.

Things were strained.

He strummed his guitar, but his heart wasn't in it. He watched her in the kitchen nodding to something on the phone, whatever it was bringing a soft smile and a faraway look to her eyes. He didn't like it, it made him nervous, jealous, worried. Was it music? A message? Was it Daniel she was talking to? He put the guitar down and went into the kitchen.

"I'll see you soon. I miss you," he heard her whisper as he entered.

It had to be Daniel. How could she miss him? Weren't they just study partners? Just friends? Just like she had told him over and over and over! He wanted to believe her, even though he had seen the way she looked when she talked to him. He had heard the gossip about how they were more, how they were sneaking around behind his back, how he was a fool, an idiot and she was cheating on him.

He stood in the kitchen and watched her, standing at the stove, stirring the pot of macaroni and cheese and the jealousy ate at him. The thought of someone else touching her, someone else kissing her, maddened him. The sight of her oblivious to him pissed him off. He knocked the phone from her grip and pushed her. Startled, her hand hit the pot sending hot water and noodles flying everywhere.

"Who the fuck are you talking to?" He demanded, mind boiling with what ifs.

"Oh my God Todd!" Her hand was scalded from the hot water; she shook it, glared at him, and ran cold water over it.

He didn't care. "Who was on the phone Jennie?"

"It's none of your business," she defended herself.

"None of my business?" He picked up the fallen pot and slammed it on the counter. "I just heard you tell someone you missed them, and it is none of my business?"

"Yes, none of your business." Her eyes hardened. "Why don't you call Brooke and whine to her about me talking to someone."

Jealousy turned everything to black, everything into lies, and he couldn't believe her. They went back and forth. The argument escalated from there. Words were flung like knives and before he knew it, she was storming out: gone.

He was so filled with rage that he did call Brooke. Truthfully, she was just a friend but she came over to talk to him, to hear him out, to calm him down and to share a bottle of whiskey. They passed out, innocently enough on the couch, which was how Jennie found them in the morning curled up, side by side.

She packed her bags, left and he didn't follow. He didn't deny any of her accusations. He wanted her to think he cheated. He wanted her to think someone else wanted him and secretly he hoped she would fight for him. Too late he realized she would take the high road and let him go. Too late he realized he should have gone after her. He should have begged her forgiveness. He should have told her he was jealous, worried, and didn't want to lose her. He should have confessed how he called Brooke to make her mad, admitted the truth. How his fear made him invite Brooke over. Most of all, he should have said he was wrong. His stubborn pride, his stupid immaturity, his dumb useless game backfired and she left.

What hurt the most was when he found out she hadn't been talking to Daniel at all but her brother Mike. By that time she was gone: gone from school, gone from her job, gone from his contacts. He never had the chance to tell her he was stupid and, most importantly, he was sorry.

****

Todd scanned the crowd and saw her talking to her friends. He knew he needed to go to her, to apologize. He also knew he needed courage, he needed the words, and it would be so much easier if he could apologize through the sounds of his guitar. Todd ordered another whiskey, downed it, and ordered another.

"Let her go Todd," Elan was saying, but he was too far gone. He had to see her. He needed to let her know how he screwed up. He ordered another shot and his head started to swim, the world tilted, and the band was still playing. Everything was wrong but right but wrong and where was she?

He saw her again, talking to a tall guy; Mr. Carmel Macchiato with a shot of espresso who had been in earlier and worn the long wool coat, the one who sat outside by himself, reading the newspaper. Todd started towards them. Jennie caught his glance, said something to Mr. Caramel Macchiato and they moved briskly through the crowd for the door.

"Todd wait—" Elan clutched at his arm, but he shook her off. Jennie. He needed to find her. He just needed to see her.

Staggering out onto the streets, the fresh air hit him like a fist, intensifying the alcohol, knocking him for a loop. He was too drunk to notice the people staring at him, asking if he was okay, clutching at him, calling his name. Todd had one thought running through his head and it was Jennie, he had to see her. To find her. He knew she would rip him apart. He had done it to her and now it was her turn. But he couldn't find her.

He didn't know where she disappeared to, which street, what car and it was too much. Clutching at a light post, he felt the cool metal beneath his grasp and collapsed against it, head pounding, the world circling like vultures pecking at him with regret. He was too late. He clutched his head, felt his heart cry out and then he was throwing up, sick all over himself, all over the ground. People were walking by and he didn't care. He rolled over on his side and wished he was dead.

Elan found him. She propped him up, helped him to his feet. Jess showed up after her with Jason and Ash from the band. They'd brought Todd's guitar, coat, a red scarf, and some towels to help clean up. Todd didn't care. He felt like death, and she was gone.

"I lost her," he whispered to Elan.

"Yeah, you did," she replied. "Sometimes you can't get the past back."

"Let me get my car," Ash said. "We'll drive him home."

Elan was right and he wanted to hate her but couldn't. He gave her the keys to his apartment and let them drive him home. He hurt. His insides, his outsides, his soul, all hurt. It was like he was losing Jennie all over again. He leaned his head against the window, closed his eyes and let his heart cry for what would never be.

****

He remembered watching her the day she had left.

Her car was loaded with all her belongings. He stood at the window looking down, half hidden by the blinds, telling himself to be strong but in reality, he was just being stubborn and doing his best to block off the pain. She was wearing shorts, a gray Washington University shirt with a flannel over it. It was an outfit that would forever be seared in his mind.

It was May and the sky was dripping tears for them.

She looked up once, paused with her hand on the door handle, her hair blowing lightly in the breeze, her eyes searching to see if he was there, if he cared. He moved back further so she wouldn't see him, hiding from her because he wanted her to come to him. Instead she got in the car and drove off.

He did nothing, watched her leave, let his hands fall from the blinds and stood there, empty, broken, lost. She wasn't coming back. He closed his eyes not sure what to do, where to turn to.

Picking up his guitar, Todd strummed a few chords, adjusted the tuning, thought of her, and started to play. The melody drifted from his heart, and it was full of sadness, depth, and ache. He poured his soul into it. When he finished with the music, he picked up a pen and started to write it down.

****

Todd wondered if she had heard *that* song earlier. The third one in their set. The one titled "Prides Regret." The one he sang the intro to over a simple melody.

"We're here Todd," Elan spoke up.

Ash helped Todd out of the car, letting him lean on Ash as they went inside. They took the elevator to Todd's floor, propping him against the wall by the door. Jess kept him from falling and even though he didn't know her that well, he was grateful. He let his words slur out a thank you.

He couldn't focus; everything appeared to be swimming. He was so lost, so drunk, so foolish.

Elan opened the door and held it, while Jason and Ash half carried, half dragged Todd in. Elan hit the lights flooding the room with brightness. He shielded his eyes. They led him to the couch where he collapsed. Jess set his guitar case on the floor and draped his coat and the red scarf over a chair. His cat, Jonesy meowed urgently, concerned. Todd picked him up and hugged him. Ash got him some water and a bowl. Jess found a blanket and covered him with it. Elan made him take two aspirin and drink some of the water. She waited to see if he would throw it back up. He didn't.

He just wanted to sleep, to curl up on the couch and let the alcohol numb him and take everything away.

"Listen Todd," she whispered, "If you need me to

stay for the night, I can." She put a hand on his arm, ever the concerned friend. "It's really no problem."

Todd rolled unfocused eyes to Elan. "I'll be fine. Swear."

"I'll check on you in the morning." She returned to the kitchen and refilled his glass with water. Jonesy was curled up next to him purring away. He felt a hand pat the blanket, felt his eyes close and drift away.

He slept like a rock.

In the morning, as dawn dug finger slivers of light across his eyelids he stirred. His mouth tasted like he had eaten a pile of sawdust. Thankfully, his head wasn't throbbing too bad. He vaguely remembered Elan and the aspirin. Smart girl. She was a good friend. He let his eyes adjust, take in his surroundings, the couch, the blanket, the bowl for him to throw up in. He rubbed his head, his beard. His body ached like he had been in a fight, beaten up, hit by a thousand waves, nearly drowned, and washed ashore as dying seaweed. He felt like shit. Literally.

Rolling over, he tried to focus on the night before. He remembered his band playing, remembered going to the bar after they finished and Elan buying him a drink. And Jennie. Shit. Jennie had been at the bar. He had gotten drunk. Wasted. Shit. Jennie. And she had been wearing the white dress and the perfume and he had wanted to apologize to her and shit. He fucked it up again. He had let her get away and been too drunk to tell her how wrong he was, how sorry he would always be. Shit.

He lay there for a moment before willing himself to move. Todd pushed himself into a sitting position. The world spun. It was almost eight. Thank God he didn't have to work until noon. He stood up and almost fell but kept himself upright. Plodding carefully into the bathroom, he cleaned himself up.

It came to him in the shower. The good ideas always did. He was thinking of her, he was thinking how she appeared like a ghost at midnight; the opposite of Cinderella who ran off before the clock struck twelve. No Jennie was there, dancing to the music and smiling while she twirled in her white dress. She had been a specter, a surreal vision from his past. He had just been too stupid and too shocked to do anything about it. But…he toweled off, got dressed, fed Jonesy, and gave him some tuna treats. Pouring himself some left over coffee, Todd heated it up and looked over at his guitar.

He knew she'd heard the song he had written for her. She had told him she had been there for his set. And he suddenly knew how he could apologize. Taking his coffee into the front room, he set his guitar free, held the instrument with care and love like it was Jennie. He ran his fingers across the strings, closed his eyes and started to play, started to create the apology he had been unable to form into words the night before.

"*It's at midnight when the secrets come out*," he sang softly before writing the tune down.

Chapter 7

Secret Lies

Jennie was surprised how much it hurt to see him. She had known he would be there but still. To walk in, see him on the stage and hear him sing; It was like a slap. And the song…God how it wounded her.

When he finished playing, she thought about leaving but didn't. She stood on the dance floor talking to her friends, Ana, Cyrus and Lola, watching him from the corners of her eyes, until Todd saw her. His eyes went wide, his mouth opened, and he stared at her.

"I'm going to say hi to Todd." Jennie leaned in close to her friend Ana.

"Good luck," Ana gave her arm a squeeze. "We'll be here if you need us."

Taking a deep breath as she walked to him, Jennie squared her shoulders, and put on a hopeful smile. She didn't know how he would react. The last time she had seen him was the day they broke up. The day she left.

"Hi Todd," She pushed her long hair to one side.

Their conversation was awkward, stilted. Words she wanted to say wouldn't come out. Instead she stuck to the basics, how are you, what's new. The guilt she felt inside was eating at her. The voices whispered tell him, tell him, but she couldn't. It was too late.

It was almost midnight when she walked away and

went back to the dance floor. She pretended she was okay but inside she felt like she was dying.

"How was it?" Ana asked.

"Weird." Jennie waved her hands dismissively, "I shouldn't have come."

"You can't avoid him forever." Lola draped an arm around her.

"I know." Jennie switched the subject and searched for her brother Mike, she wanted to leave. Where was he? Scanning the crowds, Jennie finally saw him, talking to a dark-haired man dressed in black near the patio. When she finally caught his eye, Mike took one look at her face and hurried over.

"You okay?" He put his hands on her shoulders and gazed intently at her.

"I'm fine," she lied.

"Was that him singing when we walked in?"

"Yes."

"Did you know he would be playing tonight?"

"Well…I was kind of secretly hoping he would be here so I could see how he was. I heard he was with a band I just didn't know the name of the group." She risked a glance over at Todd. He was at the bar drinking, talking with a young lesbian couple who appeared to be friends of his. He looked like his heart had been torn out and she knew she was the reason why. A sob built inside her and she placed a hand to her throat.

"Do you want to go?" Mike asked.

Jennie nodded, "Yes." She had come back to soon. Mike wrapped an arm around her and they walked out of the bar. All of the guilt she'd spent trying to forget, to bury in heaps of her soul, came seeping out. She willed herself, begged herself, not to cry.

Outside the cold smacked into her, the rain cried for her, and the city moved. Life didn't stop when your heart broke. That was the sad reality.

"Did he say anything to hurt you? Do I have to go back and defend your honor or anything? Should I be worried about him coming after us?" Mike asked as they walked towards the parking garage around the corner.

"No, he was very nice. Distant but polite. Surprised." She cast a quick look over her shoulder as they entered. She didn't see Todd following. "He may try to come after us." She wished he would. Wished he had done it before. Wished she had gone back to him in the past instead of running away, but it was too late.

They took the elevator up to the fourth floor. Mike had scored with a spot close by. He unlocked the doors to his car, opened hers, and let her inside.

"You know I go there almost every weekend. I had no idea he was the guy," he said as he slid into the driver's seat.

"Well, you only moved here six months ago."

"True."

"And it's not like I wanted to talk about it." She played with a lock of her long hair, twisting and wrapping it around her fingers.

"Are you going to be okay?" Mike glanced over at her.

"I'll be fine." Shifting in the car seat, she watched the midnight lights of Seattle fly by.

Her brother lived at The Martin on Fifth. The location was prime real estate he had paid a hefty price for, but he deserved it. He worked hard at his job at Microsoft and was recovering from a nasty divorce. The condo was payback to the bitch he never should have married. He had left her the house in Redmond. Jennie was staying with him in the spare bedroom until she could get a job and find a place closer to the University of Washington Campus.

"Did you ever tell him the truth?"

"No." She didn't want to talk about it.

It was a short drive to his building. He pulled into his assigned spot. They took the elevator to the fifteenth floor, walking down a red and gray carpet to room fifteen twenty-seven. Unlocking it, Mike flipped on the lights, dimming them from becoming too obtrusive. It was a two-bedroom two bath unit with a large window and sliding glass doors opening to a small balcony with a view of the city skyline. The walls inside were lined with black and white prints of various city scenes. In each photo was a single object in red. The furniture was black leather with red accents. A red tray with red candles sat on the kitchen island with three dangling stained-glass lights above it. Mike went to the kitchen and poured himself a shot of brandy He held up the bottle to Jennie. She nodded. He poured her one as well.

She set her handbag down on the counter, opened the sliding glass doors and stepped outside. Seattle lay before her like a sleeping jewel. The air was dripping with a light mist of rain and the sky was dark, obsidian blue, with scattered stars peeking out behind a gathering curtain of clouds. The moon was a faint crescent, a hook casting its own scant light upon the balcony, and she felt so alone. Her brother tapped her on the shoulder and held out the shot glass to her.

"To new beginnings?" He suggested.

"Yes." She touched her glass to his and shot the amber liquid back. It burned down her throat.

"You sure you don't want to talk about it?"

Jennie shook her head. "I do, but I don't," she confessed, "It's one of those things you don't think is going to hurt or mean anything and yet the act haunts you afterwards. The guilt." She looked up at him, "I see children and I wonder if I made a mistake. It's not like I can go back and undo what I did. It was a decision I made and, in the moment, when you are making it, you think it's the right one...and yet here I am thinking it was wrong."

"Did he ever know?"

"No." Her hair fell like a curtain between them.

"Mom and Dad were cool about it."

"There wasn't much they could do. The deed was done."

"Did you go crazy staying with them?"

A sad laugh escaped her. "There were moments when I thought I would lose it. Mostly they were just there in case I needed anything. We never really talked about it. You know Dad, he hates talking about anything emotional and Mom, well, all she wants to do is clean, cook, and fix things. She followed me around for the first few days checking on me, fluffing pillows, trying to get me to eat."

"Ah. Mom." He chuckled.

"Dad gave me a hundred dollars and said go buy something nice."

"That would be Dad." Mike polished off his drink, "I'm going to head to bed. I'm off tomorrow, so we can hang out, look for apartments, whatever? Hit Pikes Place or something?"

She nodded. "Sounds good."

"You know where everything is right? There are

extra blankets in the closet of your room, and the fridge is mostly full. We can get some more stuff tomorrow."

"Thanks Mike." She leaned against the rail. "Go to bed, you look beat." She forced a smile. "I'm not going to stay up to late."

"Alright, goodnight sis."

He went back inside, and Jennie resumed her contemplative study of the city.

This was a place for romance. This was the perfect setting for it. She glanced down at the street below and watched as late-night people walked by. How many of them were lovers? They were too far away to hear, too far away for details but her mind could supply the words, the jests, and the conversations.

She missed being in love. She missed the intimacy of someone else being in her life. It was only at night that she could admit such thoughts to herself. It was only at night when she felt weak, lonely, and left out. She was far too young to feel such heartache.

But seeing Todd had hurt her far more than she wanted to admit, and part of it was due to the lies she'd told, the secrets she kept from him. She had destroyed the relationship and let him think he did. That was her loss.

In her defense, she hadn't wanted him to know the truth. She hadn't wanted him to have to deal with what she discovered, the baby she was carrying when neither of them was prepared to have a baby. So she slipped away, had an abortion, and never told him. It was wrong of her in so many ways. She knew it and could only live with the choice. There was no going back and changing anything anyway. It was done. She had hurt him. She had hurt herself. And worst of all she had aborted a child she still found herself wondering what he or she would have been like.

The unborn fetus had become a ghost haunting the corners of her eyes and her mind with what-ifs. She felt tears well up and bit her lip trying to hold them back. But seeing Todd, hearing Todd, being that near to him had brought everything back and she hated herself.

She pushed the door closed and let the sobs overtake her. She didn't want her brother to hear her. He had enough going on in his life. This was her pain to embrace and cherish, this was her lie to hold close and treasure. Jennie held onto the railing of the balcony and cried. The moon slipped out from the clouds and bathed her in its light. There was no warmth in its arms. She felt empty, drained, and filled with sadness.

Drying her eyes, she went back inside. No one had told her how painful her decision would be. She had ended a life. At times she felt like a murderer. Maybe she should have gone to counseling like her parents suggested. There were a lot of things she should have done.

She poured herself another shot and went into the spare bedroom. Changing out of her white dress, she slipped into a simple cotton sleep shirt before moving into the bathroom and getting ready for bed. Her chest ached, like a great weight of sorrow was pressing down on her. She put a hand to her heart like she could hold it, like she wished she could take it out and cradle it, bandage it up, rock it to sleep, and let it know everything would be all right. She knew what it was…it was seeing Todd again after all this time, hearing his voice, smelling his cologne, watching him as he nervously tugged at his beard. Todd.

Jennie looked at her reflection in the mirror. Her gray blue eyes were ringed with dried circles of mascara. The rest of her makeup was slightly smeared. She swept her hair back from her face, saw the sadness written all over her and wished she could go back to the beginning, when she first met Todd. Wished she could rewind, correct the mistakes and fix things. But you can't change the past, only learn from it. Still to go back to the beginning…

****

They talked about staying together, getting a house, growing old, compared their dreams and goals. She told him how she wanted to be a nurse. He told her how he wanted to be a musician. Her favorite times were when he sat cross legged on the floor practicing his guitar and strumming tunes for her while she did her homework. She loved to watch him play, loved to watch the way his hands moved across the strings, the way they stroked music out of the guitar. "What?" He stopped, catching her watching. His brown eyes inviting, his laugh a song.

"Your hands are magic." She started to undress. "Can you play me like that."

He set the guitar down and took her in his arms, lighting her body on fire with his kisses, his touch, letting his hands and tongue work magic on her. He finally entered her, plunging himself deep inside, working his strokes slowly at first, letting them build with her cries, matching her moves with his body finding song and drawing it forth.

They talked about children; what they would do if they found themselves in that position. She didn't want children right away. She wanted a career, to finish school, to learn her craft, to become a nurse. He wanted to wait as well. Still they lay there on the bed one night smoking pot and talking about names.

He said, "Calvin if it's a boy."

"Calvin?"

"I've always liked that name."

She thought about it, took a drag of the joint and handed it over. "Calvin Edward Knolls." She nodded. "I like it."

"And if it's a girl?" He leaned up on one elbow and traced her bare breast, making her nipples harden with his touch.

"Scarlett," she replied, "Scarlett Ann."

"Why Ann?"

"My mother's name."

"Okay. It works." He snubbed the joint out, put his arms around her, and drew her close. "Maybe we should make a baby." He nuzzled into her neck, nibbling and licking lightly at her skin.

When the subject came up again she admitted she didn't want a child yet. They still had so much to learn of each other. He shrugged.

"Trust me," he said without hesitation or thought, "I am not ready to be a father. I still have too much partying to do. I don't want the responsibility on top of trying to make money and figure out what I want in life. A baby would just complicate things. But years from now, years and years from now, it would be a different story."

When she missed her period the next month, she remembered his words and the way he said them. She picked up a pregnancy test at the store. Unable to wait till she got home, she used the restroom and took the test. The little blue line confirmed her suspicions. She stared at the strip knowing it was a big decision, a life changing decision. It was like she was at a crossroads with only two ways to turn. Either way her future would be altered. All the way home she thought about how she would tell him. When she arrived, he was drinking, his music notes scattered around the floor mixed with empty beer cans. She could tell it wasn't the right time.

"You okay?" She asked.

"I missed the bus again." He chugged the beer, crumpled it, and threw it towards the garbage can. "Was late to work. Lost my job at Target. Thank God the coffee place was hiring. But still, I don't know if it pays enough to help with bills. Good thing we don't have children, we would never be able to afford them."

"Yeah, it's a good thing." Her voice sounded far away.

"I start tomorrow which is one bonus because the utility bill is due. Hopefully tips are great at this new place and hey, at least I don't have to wear a uniform." He sighed and looked over at her. "Everything okay?"

"Yeah, I have an assignment, a paper I need to write. I'm just thinking about how to word things."

****

She went to Planned Parenthood, they were discrete and didn't require insurance. She asked about her options and they gave her a few weeks to consider things.

It was two weeks of living hell. She wrestled with her conscious daily and he never knew her torment. Todd never caught on. They argued a bit more than usual and he was jealous of her having to meet with a partner to write her report. It was an assignment. It meant nothing. Subconsciously she used his jealousy.

After thinking things over and weighing the pros and cons she made the life altering decision for an abortion. It was the first big secret she would ever keep from him. It was also the last one. More importantly it became the nail in the coffin of their relationship.

She had the abortion two weeks before their big fight. Two weeks before he accused her of cheating on him, lost his temper, and shoved her into the kitchen counter.

****

Jennie lay on the bed and watched moonlight as it skipped across the floor, gently inching its way over to her so it could trace her skin with pale fingers.

She thought of when they first met, how it felt to be in his arms, dancing to some sad song from the eighties. What were those lyrics? Something about music, wanting to get lost, and hurting each other because they couldn't speak the words they wanted to say? She couldn't remember. She thought of the last fight, his fear of losing her, and how she knew he would feel as if he was to blame. Her relief was now guilt because she knew in her heart it was really her lie that had torn them apart. She never gave him the chance, the opportunity to help her decide what to do and for that she would always feel regret.

It took her forever to fall asleep and when she finally did it was like she fell or slipped back in time and was in bed with Todd, listening to him play his guitar. The sound soothed her, comforted her, grounded her, and she felt at home in her dream listening to him play, listening to him whisper the words, "It's at midnight when the secrets come out."

Chapter 8

Secret's Wrath

She stood in the shadows and watched as Jess and the scrawny bitch, Elan, helped the good-looking barista—what was his name? He reminded her of a golden retriever, soft wavy brown hair and trusting brown eyes—Todd! That was it, Todd. They were helping him into a car. She knew it wasn't Elan's car. Elan was far too poor to own one, even though the car was beat up enough and looked like it could have been hers. Just what the hell Jess saw in the shaved head, tomboyish bitch, Shayla didn't know. The girl was poor. She was trash. She worked as a freakin' waitress for Christ's sake! She lived in a rundown probably mice and rat infested rent controlled apartment building on Yesler. She had nothing to offer! There was nothing attractive about her. Nothing!

Shayla's mouth turned down into an unattractive snarl. Her look was pure don't-mess-with-me. Her eyes narrowed to arrow points as she watched the car cough exhaust, sputter, and pull away. She hated them, hated them both.

She stepped out from the darkness of the alley, heading back for the bar, and felt something brush at her pant leg. She whirled around.

A shapeless, bundle of indistinguishable rags held

out a dirty hand. "Spare some change miss?"

Shayla stepped out of its reach. The thing had almost clutched her, almost touched an unwashed God knows where it had been hand against her designer jeans. She recoiled from the rags, the ripped and torn coat, the blankets, and the stench of rot rolling off it. It was excrement, disgust, and vomit all at the same time. How dare it try to touch her! Her lips spread back in a sneer. She was so much better than this filth.

"Get away!" she hissed, spitting venom.

The thing shifted closer to the shelter of its wall, and she kicked at it, wishing she could stomp it, beat it, make it pay for trying to touch her. She didn't care what it was, male or female. It didn't matter. It was weak to let itself get in that situation, begging for scraps, sleeping in the streets. She never cared for weak people.

Shayla had learned at a young age that weakness got you nowhere. Determination, strength, and the simple ability to not give a shit were what mattered.

She swallowed the bile in her throat, giving the vomit a wide berth before stepping back into the red-light interior of Secrets Café. She shuddered, letting the revulsion slither off, and found a seat at the end of the bar shrouded in darkness. She flicked a strand of her long dark wig from her shoulder and recomposed herself. This day was not going her way. She just needed to focus, to think. She needed a plan, a way to make them pay.

"What can I get for you tonight?" The bartender's name tag identified him as Jay.

Shayla put on her most inviting smile, slipping it on like a mask, and replied, "Margarita on the rocks please."

"Salt on that?" He leaned slightly over the bar taking her in.

She licked her lips. "No salt." She held out her hand, "I'm Charisma."

"Jay," He took her hand and gave it a slight squeeze, "Nice to meet you."

"You too." She turned on the charm and licked her lips.

"I'll be right back." He moved off to mix her drink.

Men were so easy to lure. All she had to do was flash them the right smile, feign the right amount of interest, give them just enough attention, and they fell into her web. It was almost too easy which was why she had switched to women. The difference was women fell emotionally whereas men were hooked by a pretty package. It made the hunt more challenging.

She had thought about going after Elan the first time Jess told Shayla about the bitch. One look at the whip thin, tightly wound, androgenous woman changed Shayla's mind. Other than breaking Elan's fragile ego, there was nothing else to gain from her so what was the point. Now the man who paid her to eat the banana…he was a better target, especially now that she knew who he was, where he worked, and just what he was hiding. She took his business card out of her pocket and ran a finger across it. Mike Hadley. He would pay.

All of Shayla's victims were simply for spite, as well as monetary advances and some, as was the case of the older woman she had been using for the last year, some were for pure ruination. The man from earlier? He was for both money and ruin. It was a game to her, all a big game to satisfy her boredom. She didn't care for any of them. She just wanted to use them, hurt them, take them down and make them pay. If she could get money out of them, all the better. She saw Jay making his way back to her and strategically lowered her shirt exposing just the right amount of cleavage.

"Here you go." Jay set the drink down.

"Thank you." She pretended to search her bag for cash.

"It's okay," His eyes rose from her barely covered breasts to meet her gaze, "I've got this one."

"You're sweet," she purred and blinked at him like a doe in headlights caught under his spell, captivated by his sheer masculinity. "I was in earlier today and left a red scarf. Did anyone happen to turn one in?"

"I haven't seen anything. I can check lost and found for you if you like," he offered.

She sipped her drink, pursing her lips and opening her mouth. She took in the straw, letting her tongue peek out as she caught a drop. Shayla laughed inside as he watched. "It's okay," she shrugged. "Did I see the barista playing earlier?"

"Todd?" Jay replied, "Yes, with his band Monkeys Breath."

"They were really good." She leaned forward. He was cute, but the barista was clearly closer to Elan. "Is he single?"

A flash of disappointment showed as he took a step back. "Yes." He got the message, "Enjoy your drink."

"Thank you, Jay." She closed the book on that one.

An idea was percolating, brewing, simmering; the perfect plan. She could almost taste it. She sipped at her drink and took in the people at the bar. The band was almost done.

They were good but clearly Todd's band had them beat. Their best song was the first one they played, the ballad. This one they were wrapping up with was okay, it just lacked the emotional punch. What was the one line she liked from the ballad? Something about it hooked her, made her forget how Jess and Georgia weren't paying attention to any of the texts she'd sent. The one line sounded like it was meant for her? Oh yeah… "You know she will rip you apart." That line. It spoke to her, made her like the song. This one, was okay, but the first song? It packed an emotional one-two punch.

She took another sip and thought about Jess. Jess was supposed to stick around. They had been friends for what, five, six years now? Jess had always been there for Shayla. For Jess to just give it all up was unacceptable. Especially after everything Shayla gave up for Jess. Not that Shayla had wanted to stay in Vegas. They had both agreed on the move to Seattle. It was a starting over, Shayla just hadn't thought it would mean starting at the bottom.

Shayla stirred her drink. Their first year in Seattle was fine. Shayla had rather liked not having a past. But then it got boring. There had been something missing and one day it hit her. It was a casual flirtation at work with a guy named Shane. She flirted back, lead him on, and later accused him of sexual harassment which resulted in him being fired. Watching him leave the building gave her a sense of joy, let her realize and recognize the excitement of the hunt, the downfall of another person, was what was missing. She started to search out victims, people she could seduce, lie to, and use to her whim.

She turned to Jess each time she broke a person and proclaimed her innocence. Jess listened to her, stood by her, and held her while she cried fake tears. Jess backed her up, believed her, and fell for her lies. Until she met Elan. Then it had all changed. Jess had grown distant.

Shayla didn't notice at first, she was busy working her charms on the older woman. It wasn't until Jess approached her one sunny afternoon and confessed, admitted she was in love, that Shayla understood the situation. She remembered it clearly.

****

Jess stood near the doorway like she was ready to run. Her hair was pulled back into a tail, and she was wearing her Mariners tank top, rubbing her shoes against the floor.

"I met someone." Her voice was so small Shayla wasn't sure she heard her right.

"What?"

"I met a girl." Jess tried again, "A woman actually, her name is Elan." The words tumbled out of her like pebbles spilling from a container, "We have been dating off and on for a while."

"No." Shayla refused to believe it.

"I love her Shay. I want to be with her."

Shayla cocked her head to one side, a strange buzzing had taken up residence between her ears, a humming sound that grew and grew and grew and she said again, "No."

"Yes." Jess stared into her eyes and Shayla saw the truth. Her friend, the one constant in her life, the one she was always able to turn to, was going to leave her.

Shayla turned her back to her and walked into the kitchen. She stood there thinking about what to do, how to rectify the situation, and picked up a knife. She held it in front of her staring at the blade. Jess followed her in.

"Put the knife down," Jess whispered.

"No." This was how she would get Jess back. Shayla would cut herself and Jess would save her, and they would go away and all of this nonsense about falling in love would stop. Jess would be hers again.

She turned to face Jess and held the knife against her wrist, pressing the blade in, feeling the sharp tang of pain, watching the beads of blood swell up. It wasn't the first time she had cut herself.

Jess grabbed the knife.

They left the next day, ran off, just the two of them and things were fine, everything slipped back to the way it was before. All thoughts of the older woman and the games she had been playing were replaced by how to keep Jess.

****

And then this.

Shayla took another sip of her drink. She ran her hands around her neck feeling her flesh, the curls of the wig. The crowd was dispersing. The band had finished up and she needed to get back to the hotel she was staying at. Coldness settled into her bones, her soul. Even though her anger was a slow simmering rage she felt frozen, empty, alone. Jess was going to pay for her betrayal. Her and that bitch Elan would both pay.

Shayla finished her drink, slithered sexy smooth off her barstool, and strode into the night. The cold air of autumn danced about her and followed her like a hungry wolf. The shadows of Seattle welcomed her, embraced her as their own, they recognized her darkness, her simmering anger, her game. They wrapped arms about her as she disappeared, her wrath following behind her like a cape.

Chapter 9

Secret Heat

Monkeys Breath was playing when Nina walked in and sat at the edge of the bar. She took her cellphone out and set it down. It was after ten. The professional attire she'd worn earlier was replaced by a black low-cut dress embracing her curves like a second skin. Over it she wore a long burgundy sweater, loose and flowy, hanging past her knees, and black mid-calf lace up boots.

The bartender, Jay, took her order for a vodka cranberry. It was a simple drink, an old standby which couldn't go wrong. She crossed her legs and watched the band, recognizing the guitar player as the barista from earlier. Their music was good, the beat lively, wrapping around the crowd, enticing them to move, to dance and hunger for the lyrics.

Secrets Café was darker at night. The stage was lit up by multicolored lights, mostly red to add a little ambiance to the scene. It was one of those normal places, looking calm and coffee shop quaint during the day but at night it came alive with a pulse, like parts of it had lain dormant and were now awake.

She checked her phone again. Nothing yet. She was waiting on a message from Carlos. They had exchanged numbers after their two-hour romp at the hotel. She really didn't expect him to contact her even though he said he would. But she was curious, like a raccoon who'd found a shiny piece of tin and wanted to play with it, feel it, study it. She wanted more. Carlos was intense, a passionate lover, an artist in bed. She hadn't been looking for sex, or even a one-night stand, when she first walked past him, but then again, when the opportunity was right there, ready, willing, and eager, why not go for it? Nina didn't have time to waste on a relationship. Too much work. She had her career to think of. But sex for the simple fact of having sex was not something she frowned on.

Once a week she found herself on the prowl for something to distract her, take the edge off her day, something "strange" she could use and discard. She had to admit, Carlos did have a certain animalistic appeal. He was like a wet dream. Not her normal type at all but damn was he good in bed. He made her want more. He knew how to please a woman and she wanted him to satisfy her needs. She could give up the casual encounters for someone like him. She wondered if she could keep him as a permanent boy toy. Someone she could call up for sexual satisfaction. Men were fine with that weren't they? They used women that way, why couldn't she use one of them? Other than sex or killing spiders she really didn't need a man for anything else.

Nina Monroe had everything she wanted and she had achieved it all on her own. She worked hard growing up, graduated Valedictorian from her high school in Rexburg, got a Scholarship to Boise State, studied, poured herself into learning and finding the right internship. She wanted out of Idaho, wanted more out of life, and the best way to do that was to use her brains to get the education she needed for the job which would make her dreams come true. She was dedicated, driven and if she was truly honest with herself, a little bit cold.

But she had to be. She couldn't afford emotions. Her mother had been an emotional wreck, bouncing from one failed relationship to another, always saying this was the one who would save her and change their lives. Just the thought of her sobbing mother crying over a man was enough to make Nina sit up straighter. She'd sworn in High School she would never need a man; she would take care of herself, and her life and she would be the one in control.

So far, she'd achieved just that. She had a job as a litigator working in one of the top law firms in Seattle, plus a wonderful apartment with a gorgeous view of the bay and Pikes Place Market. It was prime real estate location. Her bank account was set with enough money to finally wardrobe herself in the clothes and shoes she had always dreamed of. Life was perfect. A bit lonely now during the holiday seasons or when she wanted to share things with someone, but perfect none the less.

And then...Carlos. Just the thought of what transpired in the hotel room earlier, made her hot. She shifted in her chair. It was two hours well spent. She took a sip of her drink. She should have ordered a shot to go with it.

Carlos worked as a cook at Bay Haven, one of the five-star Restaurants overlooking the water view. They closed at ten. He told her he would meet her after he was through. She was early. Did that mean she was anxious? God...what the hell was she getting into? She didn't even want to think about it. It was enough to know the thought of him and what he could do with his fingers and tongue and his—oh my God it had been far too long since she had enjoyed a good fuck.

She ran her fingers across the smoothness of the bar, glanced in the mirror across from her, and tucked a strand of hair back behind one ear. Her phone buzzed; it was him. Her libido woke up and started to dance. She pulled up the message:

—Find a seat in the back where it's dark.—

What did she say to that? Was it an order? Sexually she liked being ordered around. She liked being told what to do. But did he know that? Was he issuing an order? Or was he just making a suggestion? Or did he want to get busy in the back where it was dark? Shit.

She glanced around the room. There were several tables set next to the wall with dim, single lamps hanging over them. They were not in view of the band and two of them were unoccupied. Nina carried her drink to the table in the farthest corner. Surveying the crowd, she recognized a few faces, but most not at all. She saw the waitress from earlier with her arm currently draped around the shoulders of a long-haired woman on the dance floor.

Nina sat down and checked to see if she could be seen. It was dark and inconspicuous. She settled in and waited. The table featured a perfect view of the front door and the crowd. She could sit back and observe. It was a prime spot if one wanted to watch and see all.

She rotated her shoulders and willed herself to relax. She sipped her drink and tapped her foot to the music, waiting. She ordered a second drink, glanced towards the door and there he was, tall, lean, moving like a panther, a confidant, dark predator.

He searched the crowds, turned his dark eyes in her direction, saw her, and smiled. It was enough to make her wet, to make her want to spread her legs right then and there and tell him to take her. He held up a hand acknowledging her and stepped into line at the bar. She allowed herself to be content to wait until he ordered a drink. When he drew near, she stood up and gave him a hug, followed by a nervous kiss.

"Hi," she breathed. She didn't know what to say. It was one of those awkward situations. She barely knew him and yet he knew parts of her few had ever seen. He also knew how to work those parts and wake them up.

"Hi." He undressed her with his eyes and sat down, close. He put one hand around her, feeling the small of her back under her sweater.

"How was your day?" It was a stupid thing to ask, like she cared. It was just small talk which was safe and would hopefully keep her from ripping his clothes off and having her way with him. The waitress came by and dropped off her drink. She was grateful for the distraction.

"My lunch was delicious." He leaned close and nibbled at her neck, pushing the sweater and straps of her dress aside.

She closed her eyes feeling gooseflesh break out as his tongue very lightly licked across her shoulder. He moved his mouth to her ear, and she bit her lip trying not to moan, or give up her control. "I like this outfit you have on." He stroked the material with one hand.

It took her a moment to come back to earth. He already had her on fire with wanting. "Thank you."

Carlos entwined his fingers around hers, brought them to his lips, and suckled on them. "I want to peel those clothes off of you," he whispered in her ear.

She slid closer, hungrily kissed him and replied, "I

want you inside me."

"Do you?" He pushed the table over a bit and pulled her on top of him.

She could feel how hard and ready he was. She let one hand run down across his throbbing bulge and ground herself against him. Her dress rode up, but the sweater was long enough to keep her from being exposed. He reached a hand down and pushed her wet soaking panties aside, pausing just above her pussy. She could feel the heat of her bouncing off him, like a match just needing to be flicked to life.

"Do you want to do it here?" He asked.

She did. She wanted him bad.

Nina glanced around the room; everyone seemed to be caught up in their own little life and weren't really paying attention to them. They were aided by the fact the table she picked was in a darker area. But no. What happened earlier at lunch was risky enough. Nina needed to think of her job…what would happen if she got caught? She didn't want an indecent exposure ticket on her file; she had an image to uphold. They couldn't do it in the bar.

She shook her head no. "Too many eyes," she replied, "I don't want to get caught."

"I see." He leaned back all cool and collected, watching her, making her feel like a mouse.

She slipped off his lap and sipped at her drink. She was at war with herself. Part of her didn't give a damn what people thought, would have been fine if he tore her clothes off and devoured her right there where everyone could see.

The other part said no. "So, how was work?"

"I see," he nodded, "Now we are going to have small

talk like we are dating. I thought you didn't want to date?"

"I don't want to date." She narrowed her eyes.

"Small talk, meet you for a drink—"

"It was your idea!"

"I thought you just wanted sex." His eyes narrowed and the edge of his lips tilted upward in a smile as he watched her.

"I do want sex and only sex but not here where everyone can see!"

"But in the day light at lunch time is fine?" He questioned.

She dropped her mouth to argue but couldn't think of anything to say. She glared at him. He glared back. They were like two cats circling each other, hissing, and testing the boundaries. For a moment she thought about just getting up and walking away, but she didn't.

"Take off your panties Nina and give them to me," he challenged, his eyes deep with lust, daring her to defy him.

She glared tight little daggers back at him, her temper rising with her desire. He waited. She bit back a response, reached under her dress, found the edge of her panties, wiggled out of them while keeping her eyes on his, and handed them over.

He held them to his nose. "You smell good."

She didn't say anything.

"How wet are you?"

"I'm turned on," she replied.

"Taste yourself."

She sipped her drink, set it down, and brought a finger to mouth. Licking it, she lowered her hand between her spread legs. Slowly she inserted her finger, feeling the wet heat from inside, the shell soft opening of her vagina, and stroked herself. She stirred the juices before pulling her finger out and slipping it between her lips to taste the sweet, coconut nectar of herself.

"How do you taste?" he asked.

She could play this game. Nina half closed her eyes, and licked her lips. "I taste good, like honey but sweeter." She reached her hand back down, watching him. She wanted him hungry.

Carlos watched her with starving eyes, polished off his drink, and said, "We should go."

"Already?"

"Yes." He pulled her to him and roughly kissed her. "There are things I want to do to you, and you won't let me do them here."

"Oh…" Nina stood up, straightened her dress, and downed the last of her drink. Excitement pulsed in her, bringing heat to her body, awakening nerves crying out for his touch. He kissed her again, hard, lips hungry, body taut. And she took it, pressing her body against his, letting him devour her, drain her, ignite her, feeling his need match her own.

"Oh my God what you do to me." She was on fire. She wanted him inside her: his fingers, his tongue, his dick, anything…she just wanted him to fill her, to take her, to fuck her, to make her come.

Carlos laughed. "My God you are hot."

"You have no idea."

He took her by the hand and led her outside, fighting through the crowd, parting them, passing them, stepping through. They were all a blur, they were nothing to her but background noise. She walked with him down a hall past the restrooms. He grabbed a scarf from a line of coats hanging near a door, pushed it open, and they were outside.

Glancing around, Nina realized he led her out the back, not the front. She looked up, catching a glimpse of the night sky above the hovering steel buildings surrounding them. Except for the faint starlight it was dark.

He dragged her around the corner to the alley, pushed her against the wall. Shifting her legs apart, Carlos slipped his fingers inside her. The wall was rough, abrasive, his fingers relentless, pushing, probing. He wrapped a hand around her neck holding her in position, rubbing her clit and Nina cried out. She could feel the fire in her build. Her hands fluttered, reaching for his cock, undoing his zipper.

"Inside me. Please." The need, the hunger, was primal. It peaked and made her beg.

Carlos obliged, withdrew his fingers, stuck them in her mouth and let her lick them before thrusting his penis deep inside her hungry vagina. It was sharp, sudden. Leaning back, Nina wrapped her legs around his waist. She felt the wall digging into her back, through the sweater, through the dress, and wished she was naked. She didn't care about the scratches, she didn't care about the wall, she didn't care about anything. She just wanted him to fill her, to drive himself deep inside her, ride her, slam into her, and take her. He pumped away, pounded into her pussy giving it everything he had and more. She clasped onto him, holding him tight, feeling the roughness, the coldness of the air. Suddenly she felt a push, a release, like a water balloon bursting. Liquid gushed out of her, flowing in spurts, and she gasped in his ear, holding on for dear life.

"Holy shit." He was taken aback. "Are you...? Did you just pee?"

"No," She disentangled herself from him and stood on shaky legs, "Did I squirt? Oh my God, I'm sorry."

"Sorry?"

"Yes, it can be a bit messy."

"Does this happen often?" He reached a hand out to her, gently touching her face.

"Only if I have gotten off a few times in a row." She tugged her dress down.

"And then what?"

"I don't know." She gave a nervous laugh. Her legs were soaked. Her shoes were soaked. "Shit, I probably got you all wet, didn't I?" She felt his jeans and they were soaked.

"It's okay. They will dry."

Nina bit her lip. She felt like she had killed the mood. She leaned against the wall and caught her breath. Liquid was still dripping down her legs. She wished she had something to wipe it up with, to clean herself off with.

"Are you okay?" His voice was tender, concerned. His touch gentle.

"I'm fine. Just wet." She stood up straight and wrapped her sweater about her, using the bottom half to dry off her legs.

"Here." He took the scarf he had grabbed and helped her clean up.

"I need to go home and change." Nina pushed a lock of her hair away from her face.

"Not yet." He ran his fingers along her jawline and tenderly, slowly, kissed her, drawing her into his arms. "I want to taste you first." He whispered, and she shivered.

"Oh…" between kisses, feeling his urgency grow, feeling him harden again, feeling the small quakes between her legs, "Okay."

"We need to find a better place though." He held her close and glanced around the alley they were in.

She was still trying to get her bearings. Her legs were weak. Her heart was recovering. Her vagina was throbbing, swollen, as if it had its own heartbeat. Carlos took her hand and led her further behind the buildings. She wasn't sure what he was looking for until she saw the pickup truck parked in the back like it belonged to someone who worked nearby. It was shrouded in shadows, hidden.

"Perfect." He whispered, glanced around to make sure they were safe and unobserved.

Nina watched as he carefully eased the tailgate of the truck down, took his jacket off, laid it on the cold metal, and helped her up so she was facing him. She took her sweater off and rolled it into a ball for a pillow. The air was cold enough to snow, but her skin was warm. He set the scarf to the side, pulled her dress down exposing her breasts to the moonlight.

Carlos lowered his lips to a nipple, biting it, stroking it, slipping a hand back between her legs like it was his home and she welcomed him. She reached for his hard on. He pushed her hands aside, raised her legs to either side of his shoulders and thrust his fingers in faster. She clutched at the edge of the pickup, frantic for something to grab onto. He let his tongue trace her clit and lap at her labia. She moaned and dug her fingers into his hair. He pulled back for a moment perhaps remembering how she had gushed and removed his shirt.

In the scant light of night, he was a sculpted vision of heat. His eyes met hers, a life link, a tether, tying them together before he squatted down and buried his tongue inside, tasting her nectar. The licks were soft against her swollen and bruised vagina; She opened herself to him. He found her clit with his teeth and nuzzled it, not biting, but waking it slowly before adding a couple of fingers, slipping one into the tightness of her butt as well, working the two openings together.

Nina was on fire, there was only pleasure, only desire, only this hungry need to be satisfied. She could not get enough of him. Her entire body and mind were under his control. She gave herself to the sensation, to the fire burning inside. She felt her pleasure build, mount, burn, like lava, like liquid heat wanting to explode, to pour out. She gave a primal moan as he struck just the right spot and pushed it and that was it right there, oh God, that spot. Her back arched and it gushed out of her again, a stream, a river, an ocean, a crescendo of waves upon waves of storm ridden pleasure. She bucked and he held her, drinking her in, tasting her. It was intense, her senses blinked, everything shifting from dark, to light, like stars were exploding into supernovas.

At last she gasped for breath and begged him to stop. He leaned back, licked his lips and the night smelled of musk, coconut, heat, and sex. He picked up the scarf and wiped his face clean. She was still shuddering, the metal of the truck cooling the embers of her fire.

"I am so, so glad I followed you inside earlier." He gathered her exhausted body close and held her, helping her get her sweater back on.

Nina wrapped her arms around his neck, feeling

their hearts pounding a synchronized beat. "So am I," she replied.

They relaxed in the nights embrace. The cool air wrapped around them, feeding on the moist sweat of their skin, the wet stickiness of their cum. The city was a blanket of soft noise, faint cars, quiet voices and the music thumping from inside Secrets. They were both soaked and spent, and she wanted more but didn't think she could take it. She lay curled up in his arms like a cat; a soft, delicious, incredibly sexy cat.

"Let's get you inside," he helped her to her feet, "Can you walk?"

"Yes." She kept her arm around his waist "I do need liquids though, a drink, water, a cocktail, something." She let out a short laugh. She was going to hurt in the morning. Hell, she hurt already.

"Drinks then." He opened the door, draped the scarf over the nearest coat, and they made their way back to the bar.

The first band had just finished playing. A short, slim bald man with glasses was on stage thanking them and getting the crowd geared up for the second group. They made their way through the throngs of people and found a spot at the edge of the bar. Carlos signaled to the bartender who acknowledged them with a nod.

"What do you want to drink?" He asked.

"Vodka Cranberry." She gingerly sat down.

He ordered two while Nina checked the crowd out. Secrets was pulsating with people, it was a packed house filled with a variety of voices in conversation, noise and the vibes of good times. She wondered if anyone other than their former waitress could sense or even smell they just had sex. Surely it must be in the air. She was wet.

Her hair was matted and there was dried cum on her legs. She could feel it. She drew in a deep breath and excused herself.

There were two stalls in the women's bathroom. One of them was occupied. Nina stepped up to the sink and got a couple paper towels wet. She cleaned off her legs. She took her long sweater off and brushed the debris from it, noticing a rip near the bottom, probably courtesy of the wall. Straightening her dress, Nina ran her fingers through her hair, trying to give it some semblance of order, style. She looked like she had just been fucked by five men. Her skin was flushed, her lips full, bruised. Nina leaned in close to the mirror took her lipstick out of her sweater pocket and applied it to her lips.

She needed to get herself back. She needed to recompose. The sex had been incredible. Wonderful! Releasing! But it was just sex she reminded herself, only sex and that was all it could ever be. Just an affair. Just an incredible, hot, mind-blowing sexual affair.

A raven-haired woman emerged from the locked stall, glanced at Nina in the mirror before a lock of curling darkness obscured her from view.

"Nice dress, Nordstrom's?" The woman commented.

"Yes, thank you." Nina replied and dismissed her. The woman left, glancing back once and Nina wondered if there was something on the dress. Was there dried cum? Was it torn? She checked it out with her hands since the mirror only showed her flushed face.

Her mind was coming back to her. She needed to put Carlos in his place. Squaring her shoulders, she walked back to the bar.

Carlos handed her drink to her. She took a sip. "I should go after this," she said.

"Done with me already, hmmm?" Carlos looked at her from his liquid eyes.

"Beat," she replied, "Just beat."

"So, no round three?"

"Not tonight," she looked away, "Don't think I could take one more."

"Let me walk you home." He traced her chin line.

Nina closed her eyes. His touch was electric velvet. She had to be strong.

"No," she shook her head, "No. I'm sorry. I…"

"I understand," he removed his hand, leaned back in his chair, and shrugged, "Just sex. Just an affair."

He understood. Thank God! For a moment she had been worried. She finished her drink and stood up, straightening her dress with one hand.

"You're a wet dream come true Carlos," she whispered as she kissed him, "But nothing more."

He slid off his chair and pressed her hard against him, "Is that so?" He reached between her legs, right there, at the bar, with everyone around them. She pushed a hand against his chest, his sexy, young, delicious chest, trying to get away. He held her close, bruising her mouth with his lips while he fingered her. She felt exposed, turned on, like an animal trapped by his desire. She fought for a moment, before giving in, and just like that he released her.

"Enjoy your night, Nina." He turned away and sat back down, "You know how to reach me."

It took her a moment to get herself together. He had dismissed her, left her burning, wanting, and backed off like he didn't care. She didn't know what to say. She did know what to do though. Squaring her shoulders, hoisting her sweater tighter about her, she moved through the crowd like she owned it and walked out into the night. *You know how to reach me?* Arrogant bastard.

The night was crisp, the smell of rain hovered in the air, and the two blocks to her apartment complex passed in what felt like seconds. She stabbed a finger at the elevator button, tapping her foot the entire ride to her floor.

Nina was turned on and pissed at the same time. How dare he? Unlocking her door, she stepped inside, setting her key in a little dish she kept on the long narrow table in the entry. Flipping on the overhead lights, Nina reached in her pocket, took out her wallet, lipstick, and cellphone. The later, vibrated with a message.

She ignored it glancing around her condo. It was immaculate, clean, organized, like a picture in a magazine except for her kitchen which was filled with old cooking utensils, bowls, and recipe books. Nina liked to cook when she was stressed or upset. For a moment she thought of taking her frustrations out on a batch of cookies, but it was late.

Instead, she poured herself a drink and walked to the windows dominating the entire front wall, with a view of the apartment complex across from her and a small view of the bay. She thought of his touch. Already she wanted him. He just had that way about him.

Her phone buzzed again. She picked it up:

—*Looking forward to next time*—

She set the phone down. She was spent. She was beat. She was pissed off. But she wanted him. Before she could change her mind, she texted back:

—Monday at three?—

Chapter 10

Secret Realization

The day drew the curtain down and surrendered to the night. Elan clocked out, put her coat on, wrapped the red scarf she'd found around her neck, and stepped out into the chilly embrace of the city. Her breath puffed up like little smoke signals. She walked down the alley, past Eli's truck, and onto Union Street. She thought about getting on the bus but wanted to make a stop first.

Heading to Pike's Place Market, she texted Jess she was on her way.

Jess—*See you at home*—

Home. It was a word Elan didn't know too well. Her childhood had not been a happy one. She was the youngest of three children. As far as she knew, her older two siblings looked on her with nothing but resentment. Her parents looked on her as just another mouth to feed. Her father was an abusive drunk. Her mother ignored all her offspring and spent most of her time shopping or gambling. Elan remembered many nights scrapping and digging for food from garbage bins behind the restaurants in Snohomish. Holidays were not celebrated. It was a bleak and gray upbringing which did not match any picture or description of the word home. Now, hearing the word spoken aloud, sensing it staring her in the face, she was scared, nervous, and unsure.

Home.

At twenty-four years old, Elan had never been in a serious relationship. There was too much of a chance a lover would leave her, abandon her, or hurt her, like her family. She dated a few women, but Jess was the first one Elan ever dared to want to go further with. The first one she wanted to chance facing her fear over. It was unchartered territory and scared as she was, Elan was going to navigate it. She was willing to give her heart to someone. She was willing to discover what people called home.

She crossed the street to Pikes Place Market. Some of the shops were starting to close. The Fishmongers were sweeping the floors and packing the seafood up. She stopped at one of the few open flower booths and picked out a bouquet with a large fire colored Dahlia surrounded by red and orange mums. It whispered of Jess. She paid for it and started towards her apartment on Yesler Way, turned left at the pergola on Pioneer Square, and walked the two blocks to her fixed income building.

Taking the rickety elevator to the fourth floor, Elan strode down the narrow hallway with its ratty carpet, to her unit. When she got to her door, she stood, wondering what to do, feeling her heart pound in her chest. This was it. This was the threshold she was about to cross, and it didn't matter that it was her apartment. What mattered was Jess was inside, and had been since six.

Elan pressed her head against the door and drew in a breath. From inside she could hear the faint sound of Jess singing. Elan knocked, hoping Jess would hear her. A moment later the door was opened, and Jess stood silhouetted against the white string lights. Her hair was pulled back in a loose tail. Two suitcases and a few boxes were still in the hallway.

"Hi." Elan bit at her lip and held the bouquet of flowers out to her. "Remember this morning when I said I wanted to buy flowers for you…well, I don't have a vase." She licked her lips. "But there is a glass we can use in the cupboard over the sink."

Jess took the flowers and sniffed at them, "Thank you, they are beautiful."

"You're beautiful." Elan wrung her hands together as she shut the door. She glanced down at the boxes and suitcases. Jess followed her gaze and started down the hall.

"I just brought my stuff over. I hope you don't mind. I just didn't…" Jess let the thought trail off, "I wasn't sure where I should put it."

Elan took her coat off, hung it, and looked around her small apartment. It was barely over four hundred square feet and while she didn't own a lot of belongings it was a tight fit. It could work though. "We will just have to figure it out." She nodded to herself.

Jess had been to the apartment before but never for a sleep over. This was more permanent. This was big. Elan realized there was some adjusting needed. It was one thing to think of living with Jess, it was another thing for it to happen.

"Well," Elan said, "Let's see what we can do." She winked at Jess. "First off, your coat can hang on the rack by the door, or in the bedroom closet." She led Jess to the bedroom with her double bed and two mismatched nightstands. Her bed was covered in a multicolored patchwork velvet quilt she'd found at a secondhand store. Pretty much everything in her apartment was either a hand me down from Eli, Todd, and other co-workers or a find at a thrift store. Her taste was eclectic and mixed, even though nothing matched it had an odd flow to it. In short, it worked because Elan worked, and she had an eye for putting the right complimentary color or object next to another one.

She opened her closet door and pushed her small amount of clothing to one side. "You can hang your stuff on this side." She pushed her three pair of shoes under her clothes. She went to her dresser, moved her collection of Vampire books to one end, "You can put your jewelry here." She opened the four drawers and consolidated her clothes in the bottom two. "These two drawers should work for now, right?"

"Yes." Jess swallowed.

Elan turned to the bed and narrowed her eyes, studying it. She liked to sleep on the left side. "What side of the bed do you like?"

"The right."

"Perfect." Elan beamed at her, "I like the left."

If she didn't dwell on the weird feeling of having to combine her solitary life with another person, it became more like a puzzle, how to fit her stuff with Jess's belongings. How to mesh two lives into one. Wasn't that what one did as a couple? She didn't let herself overthink, she shut her brain and its questions down and focused on the now, on what needed to be done. She turned to Jess who was still holding the flowers in her hand.

"Let me get a glass for those." Elan reached for them.

Jess held the bouquet close to her heart, focusing on them. "I was worried," she whispered.

"Worried? Why?"

"Well, you haven't lived with anyone, and I have only lived with the…her and I didn't know how it would go. Or how it will go, and I really, really want it to work."

Elan leaned in close and kissed Jess softly, she didn't want to tell Jess how worried she was as well. Relationships were something Elan didn't know a lot about. "Can I tell you something?"

"Sure."

"I want it to work too…really. I mean, it's one thing to say but another to do it and I…I want to do this with you."

"Me too." And there was the smile Elan had fallen in love with.

"Put your stuff away and I will put these in some water." Elan moved into the small kitchenette area, opened one of the cupboard doors, and took out a tall purple glass. She filled it with water and arranged the bouquet. Setting it on her little bistro table with its mismatched chairs, she placed it in the center.

For the first time she noticed music playing. When Elan wanted music, she would set her cellphone in a bowl to make it sound louder. Searching the living area, she saw a turntable set up on a corner table with three legs, one supported by coasters.

"You have a turn table?" It was an obvious statement made with awe, reverence.

Jess poked her head out of the bedroom, "Yes, I have a whole collection of eighties alternative music. I hope you don't mind."

"Mind? I'm simply happy to have something to listen to. And I *love* alternative."

"Is the stereo okay right there?" Jess stepped out of the room, "I wasn't sure where to put it."

"It's good." Elan glanced around the room and realized it was perfect: the soft glow of the string lights, the music, the sight of Jess standing there. It was like a scene from a movie, one of those perfect moments to be saved to the subconscious and played back later. Mentally shc recorded it, drank it in, and realized even though it terrified her in some way, it made sense in another.

"Would you like a drink?" Elan asked.

"Sure." Jess tucked a strand of hair behind one ear.

Elan took out two shot glasses, filled them with cinnamon flavored whiskey and handed one to Jess.

"Cheers," she said and held the shot glass out, "To new beginnings."

Jess clinked her drink to Elan's and downed the shot. Elan set her empty glass down and reached for Jess, pulling her into an embrace, kissing. Elan let herself drown in the taste of Jess, the feel of her. The music was a pulse in the background like their heartbeats had combined and created their own sound.

Elan let her fingers run across Jess's curves like she was opening a book for the first time, a story she always wanted to read and now she could not wait to open it and dive in.

And just like that, in a swirl of clothes, of light, of motion, of heat they were undressed and on the blue velvet loveseat. Jess pushed Elan back, leaned between her legs and Elan willed herself to relax. Working her tongue around Elan's vaginal walls, Jess got her good and wet, before slipping a finger into her moist cleft. Elan felt exposed, open, hungry, wet.

She spread her legs further, closed her eyes and was getting into the groove when the thoughts came, knocking unbidden on the moment. Like how much time did they have? Was it after nine? What if Todd played first? Did she smell? She hadn't used the restroom or cleaned herself up. What if she did smell? What if she tasted bad? She usually taste tested herself before having sex but she had been caught up in the moment and now Jess was between her legs. She was licking Elan, moving her tongue up and down, soft tender strokes and it felt good, but it wasn't urgent enough. Elan needed to shut her mind up.

"Stick a finger in," she whispered, thinking it would work, but the angle was wrong. She was too high up. "Let me scoot down." She was throwing the rhythm off. Shit. Relax, she told herself, just relax. Drawing in a deep breath, she pushed her thoughts aside, let her body focus on the sensation of Jess touching her, of this being the first time they would have sex as partners in *their* place and just like that she knew it wasn't going to happen. The angle was off, the timing wasn't right, and then, a cramp. She reached over kneading at her upper thigh, but it didn't work. Elan tried to ignore it, to focus on the pleasure, but the cramp intensified.

"Wait," Elan wanted to cry, "I have a cramp, I'm sorry."

Jess leaned back and her eyes betrayed her disappointment. She licked at her lips.

Elan sat up clutching at the edge of the loveseat and straightened her leg out. She glanced over at the clock. It was after nine.

"I'm sorry babe." She cupped Jess's chin and kissed her, "It's not you, really, it was feeling so good until I got this cramp."

"It's okay," Jess replied and stood up, reaching for

her shirt. "We should probably get ready to go anyway." She smiled but Elan could feel the disappointment like a heavy blanket between them, she didn't like it. It shifted the feeling of rightness to a sensation of unsure.

She reached for her underclothes and pants. "The first band goes on at ten."

"Who plays first?" Jess asked and found her own pants.

"Eli does a coin toss to see. Tonight we have Todd's band, Monkeys Breath, up against Void," Elan replied, "You remember Todd? He's the barista, the one with the brown hair? You spoke to him earlier?"

The memory of Todd telling her Jess wanted to talk to Elan came forward in her mind like a clip from a movie. The whole day was a rollercoaster ride of ups and downs. Elan stood up. She held a hand out to Jess and pulled her upright.

"I'm sorry I didn't get off." Her eyes pleaded earnestly with Jess's brown ones, "It's not you, honestly. It was the cramp."

Jess put a finger to her lips, "It's okay, we'll try again later."

"Later yes." Elan kissed her, "I'm going to get a clean shirt." She held up the one she had worn earlier. "This one smells like food."

Jess leaned in and sniffed. "You're right. Better change, you smell like something good to eat."

Elan threw the shirt at her. Jess ducked and laughed. Elan scowled but smiled, went into the bedroom to dig through her drawers for a clean shirt. She settled on one of her favorite black tees with an old rock band logo on it. She slipped into a pair of boots and stepped back into the main room.

Jess was waiting in the hallway with her coat on, looking down at her phone, the light illuminating her face. Elan knew it must be the bitch. She bit her lip from saying anything even though inside a little worm of worry began to dig a hole. She reminded herself that Jess had chosen her. Weren't those Jess's boxes and suitcases sitting in the hallway waiting to be moved in? Hadn't Jess just put some of stuff away in the closet and in the drawers? Still, the little worm of doubt whispered, *it could just as easily go the other way.*

"Everything okay?" Elan asked, reaching for her coat.

"Shayla." Jess shoved the phone in her pocket. "Mind games." She shook her head and reached for Elan's hand, "Let's go."

It was a quick ten-minute walk to Secrets. The night was chilly with the humid whisper of rain threatening to fall. They were cold, but hand in hand wrapped in the budding blossoming warmth of young love, they didn't feel it.

A block away from Secrets Café, they could hear the pulse of the music. The door was open when Elan and Jess shouldered their way into the bar. Monkeys Breath was already playing. The crowd was eating it up. They got in line for drinks as Todd gripped the microphone and started to sing one of the bands favorite "get the crowd pumped" songs. It was a good choice.

"Are we going to be able to find a seat?" Jess practically had to yell in Elan's ear.

"May have to stand for a bit." Elan scanned the area.

"I'm cool with that."

"I'm going to check the other side, see if we get lucky. Can you order me a beer?"

"Sure," Jess shrugged out of her coat, draping it over one arm

"Thanks." Elan gave her a quick kiss before moving around the corner of the bar.

Glancing back, she watched Jess take her phone out, peer at it, and return it to her back pocket. The doubting worm tried to dig its way to the surface, but Elan shoved it back into the dirt.

She wove her way between the crowds searching for a table, but her mind was on the phone calls. What was the bitch saying? Was she trying to weasel her way back in? Was she plotting something? She had to be. Elan gave up the search and walked back to where Jess stood holding two beers.

Todd was on his third song, a slow one. He stepped back from the microphone and strummed a single note, letting it vibrate and fade into memory. He spoke softly, and it was an apology to a ghost from his past. Elan recognized it as the song written for his ex, the one who had gotten away. The words were a magical mixture of teardrop memories and sadness.

"Holy shit." Jess whispered, "He is good. And so emotional. Did he write this?"

"Yes." Elan replied, "It's an apology to his ex."

"Damn." Jess turned to her and wrapped her arms around her neck, "It is so sad. What happened?"

"He doesn't talk about it much. All I know is it hurt him very deeply and he blames himself." Elan held her close and trailed kisses down her neckline.

Thankfully, the next song had a happier beat. Reaching for Jess, Elan took her out to the dance floor. They stepped and swayed to the music and found their groove. Their bodies responded to the music in a synchronized blend of belonging. It wasn't long before Todd announced the final song.

"We should buy him a drink," Jess suggested as they picked up their beers from the edge of the bar and finished the last drops.

"Good idea." They got back in line, "Let me go meet him and tell him where we are."

"Okay." Jess leaned in for a kiss, "I'll hold down the fort."

Elan started to walk away. She wished again that there was some way to record the moment, capture the magic of it. Everything felt so surreal: Jess here with her, the music a splash of background, the lights, the crowds, it was perfect. She glanced around the bar, taking everything in, wanting to memorize the scene of their first night out as a couple.

From the corner of her eye, she saw Jess in line behind a red headed woman. Elan recognized her as the woman who came in and wrote in a notebook while she sat by herself. As Elan watched, both the red head and Jess took their phones out, glanced at the little screen that dominated everyone's world, stared at whatever message was on the screen and simultaneously put their phones away. It was odd in the exactness of the moment. It stole from the magic and brought the worm of doubt crawling back from the hole Elan had banished it to.

It could only be Jess's ex-roommate Shayla, but if it was, why was the red head reacting the same way. What were the odds of two people giving the same attention to a message on their phones and ending it in the same amount of time? Was the red head the ex? Was the world really that small? Had Elan been waiting on Shayla all this time and not known it? No. Jess had told her Shayla went to school with her, and the red head was older, maybe in her late thirties or early forties, but definitely older than twenty-three.

Elan snuck back into line and kissed Jess. "I should wait till the song ends," she whispered, "I don't want to be away from you for too long." Jess still held her phone in her hand. Elan looked down at it and asked, "Was that her?"

Jess didn't deny it.

"Do we need to worry?" Elan asked.

"No, she can fuck off." Jess replied, "I'm going to block her number. I'm done with her shit." She hit the button, finalized her resolve, and put the phone in her back pocket. She slipped her arm into Elan's and moved closer, "This is our night, the beginning of the rest of many a night together and I am tired of her interruptions."

Monkeys Breath wrapped up their last song and the crowd erupted in cheers. Elan passed Jess a ten, "I'm going to go congratulate him, would you order me another beer?"

"Sure," Jess replied.

Elan moved through the crowd and fought her way to the end of the stage.

"Is that your girl?" Eli, her boss, asked as they crossed paths, nodding back to the line where Jess stood.

"Yes." Elan followed his gaze.

"I can see why you were late," Eli joked and beelined for the stage.

It was a silent but welcome approval, and meant a lot to her. Eli was like a father to her in more ways than one. He had been there for her, helped her out, taken her in when she had nowhere to go, given her a job, helped her find a place to live. His approval and forgiveness all in one sentence made her feel safe and reassured, like things were right with the world. She watched him step onto the stage and thank Monkeys Breath. She watched Todd and his crew take a final bow before starting to undo, unplug, and dismantle their equipment for the next band.

At the moment, the world felt like it couldn't contain any more perfection, any more memories needing to be saved and stored in the confines of let's play this one back when we need to see how magic works.

Later, after Todd's meltdown, after his sighting of Jennie, after his one too many drinks, after dropping him off at his place and having his band mates Ash and Jason drive her and Jess home, later Elan would replay those feelings and wonder how the world could tilt from one emotion to the other. What would stand out to her the most was how unphased Jess was, how she had stepped up and was there without hesitation or question.

When they unlocked the door to the apartment, Elan stood for a moment. "I will need to get you a key." She said and it hit her, this was now their home.

Their place.

She turned to Jess, and everything crashed, collided, and embraced. Elan clutched at Jess, kicked the door shut and amidst a whirlwind of touching, fumbling for buttons, zippers, removal of any and all clothing acting as barriers between them, they found themselves in the bedroom, *their bedroom.*

This time when Jess pushed Elan back on the bed, when Jess settled between Elan's legs, lifting one, running soft fingers down her calf, burning her touch like a brand into Elan's skin, this time Elan relaxed into it.

She felt on fire. She felt every finger, every caress, every soft velvet stroke. When Jess trailed her tongue lightly down Elan's leg, tickling the back of her knee, bringing chills to her skin, Elan laughed and fought to break free, but Jess wouldn't back down. She spread Elan's legs, slipped a finger inside the smooth wet shell like opening of Elan's nether mouth. Jess caressed it, cupped it, and teased it with gentle strokes, building into a rhythm, a pattern, a chord strumming from Elan's clit to her heart, to her soul and Elan cried out.

She forgot everything but Jess's touch, the way her fingers moved as if they belonged, like they were part of Elan, coaxing her, bringing her to life. Jess scissored her fingers back and forth, two of them inside, her thumb pressing on Elan's clit, rubbing, coaxing. She lowered her mouth, tongue flickering out, wet heat licking at the velvet trail between clit and opening, and Elan bucked under the difference. It was fire, water, lava meeting the ocean, waves: moving, crashing and burning with pleasure.

The combination of Jess's fingers and tongue brought Elan to the edge, made her see a kaleidoscope of colors, patterns and it was back and forth, ice and fire, explosions, supernovas bursting, fireworks flaring, nerve endings singing. She was shuddering, she was crying, she was clutching at the fingers buried in her hair, tugging at them, calling out and gasping, pleading stop don't stop right there and yes yes yes oh God, yes right there, right there and a flood, a waterfall. And she was done, coming down, sliding, peeling herself out of the skies and falling to earth. Done.

"Stop." Elan gasped, rolled over on her side, her body shone with perspiration. She felt alive and spent all at the same time.

Jess leaned back, wiping a hand across her face, licking her fingers, and lay beside Elan. Jess reached out and took her hand and Elan knew they could work, they would work. If she kept her fears away, if she pushed her doubts aside and let herself trust, relax into the now, the relationship would grow. She realized she could do this. They could do this.

Chapter 11

Secret Denial

When Mike parked in the garage near Secrets Café, he looked over at his sister. Jennie was chewing on her lip and huddled into the side of the passenger seat.

"Are you sure you want to do this?" He asked for what felt like the hundredth time.

"Yes. I think it would be fun."

But her voice sounded forced to him.

He turned the car off and got out. He had been to Secrets Café earlier in the day, before his sister had arrived in town, before she had gotten settled in and asked if they could go out.

"I saw on the internet they do this battle of the bands thing and I want to check it out." She shut the door.

"Aren't you tired though?"

"No. Besides, it would do you some good to get out at night."

She had a point. It had been what? Eight months? Nine months since the divorce from she who must not be named. He had hidden out for a few, and when the divorce was finalized, he treated himself to the two-bedroom two-bath condo unit at The Martin on Fifth. Mike had lived there for six months, existing on the basics of survival, eat, work, walk, and repeat.

It wasn't until recently he even dared to venture out

further then his day-to-day routine. He had started going to Secret's Café on the weekends when he was off, to enjoy a caramel macchiato and some breakfast. It was his treat to himself in more ways than one. He had not been to Secrets at night. In fact, when he thought about it, he hadn't been out anywhere since he moved into the city. It was a waste of a good time.

So, he let her talk him into it and now they were here.

****

The music was pumping out the door. A couple of people were standing in front smoking. Jennie smiled, but she wasn't fooling him. He knew she was nervous. He just didn't know why. She still carried a sense of fragile brokenness about her, but it was smaller. He knew she'd left Seattle because she was heartbroken. He knew it had taken her a while to recover from the abortion and the pain. He knew their parents had helped her heal and he knew she was now ready to face her past and live again.

Grief and guilt did that to a person, made them seek comfort in solitude. He should know. Hadn't he been doing the exact thing for the past six months? Although he wasn't hiding from grief or guilt, he was hiding from a secret.

A secret no one knew, not even his sister, and definitely not his ex-wife.

Mike followed Jennie inside. Secrets Café was ignited by red string lights, giving the room a much more intimate and furtive look. Unlike during the day when only the corners were shadowed, most of the room at night was obscured and closeted. It was packed with people, overlaid with conversations and music. The first of the two bands was already playing on stage.

Directing Jennie to the line for drinks, Mike took in the setting and wondered if there was anyone from the day who might recognize him. He spotted the barista from the morning shift playing the guitar which was a surprise. But who knew what anyone did behind closed doors or when they were out of their uniform and living their non-work life? Everyone had a secret.

"Have you been here before?" He asked Jennie.

"Not for a long time." A faraway look in Jennie's eyes made him wonder if she was seeing old ghosts. "I used to come here." She scanned the room, "It really hasn't changed much."

"I'm usually here on the weekends." Mike shrugged out of his overcoat.

He didn't add how he recently started to pay people to eat food in a suggestive manner while he watched. It was something else he did not want his sister to know.

Mike draped his coat across his arm; He should have left it in the car. Too late for that though. God, when was the last time he'd gone out on a Friday night? It had to have been with she who must not be named, his big mistake—the controlling, nagging, demanding bitch he married as a cover, to hide who he really was.

The harpy had her own issues. Beside her need to be in control, she didn't like to eat anything and was obsessive about working out. She had this insane notion that one ounce of fat was a bad thing. Frankly, in Mike's opinion, an ounce or two or even a pound or two of fat would have improved her cadaver looks. But when he found out about the nineteen-year-old she was fucking while he was at work, it gave him the excuse he needed to end things.

God, the kid was almost thirty years younger than she was. It was just sick and wrong and sick and…he shook his head in disgust at the thought. The harpy liked them young. Hell, he was fifteen years younger, but *thirty*? Well, whatever, let the jobless kid who still lived at home with his parents have her. They could move in together and she could finally have the child she always wanted…in more ways than one. It was gross. But hey, at least it gave him the out he needed. She tried to ask for more in the divorce but once Mike's lawyer brought up the barely of age man she was having a love affair with, she changed her tune.

"What can I get you?" The bartender interrupted his thoughts.

"Mike?" Jennie bumped his shoulder.

"Oh, sorry. I'll have an old fashioned."

"I'll have a cosmopolitan," Jennie added.

Mike dumped his brain of any memories of his ex. He never should have married her and that was the bottom line. At least her infidelity freed him from paying any alimony. She got the house, and the four thousand a month rent, plus the lovely utility bills. Karma, bitch, karma. Of course, if she'd found out his secrets, it might have gone a different way.

He sipped at his drink and directed Jennie towards the end of the bar and two available chairs. Jennie suddenly stiffened next to him. She was staring at the guitar player, the barista from earlier. Todd, wasn't that his name? He was singing a slow ballad.

"You okay sis?"

She nodded, but didn't reply. Her mouth was open, gaze fixed on the singer.

"Oh my God! Jennie?" A blonde woman sang out

and pushed her way over to them.

It was Mike's turn to nudge his sister, "Jennie." She turned just in time to catch the woman's embrace.

"Ana? Wow."

"It's been what? A year?"

"Little more, but who's counting?" Jennie gave her a hug, "Who are you here with?"

"Lola and Cyrus." Ana replied, "We are here to support…" her voice trailed off. "Does he know you are here?"

Jennie shook her head no. She turned back to Mike, introduced him, and asked if he was okay with her going to say hi to a few old friends. He was fine with it. Draping his coat over her chair, he sat down and wondered who the "he" was the Ana chick referred to. Jennie had suggested Secrets. Did she know the barista?

"Excuse me, is someone sitting there?"

Mike looked up into a pair of dark eyes. It was hard to tell in the red lights if they were brown or deep blue. Mike took in the black haired perfectly built man standing before him and swallowed. The man was dressed in a red and black button-down shirt tucked into black denim form fitting jeans. Mike swallowed again, bringing his eyes back from the mental undressing.

"I'm sorry…what?" He stammered knowing he sounded like an idiot.

"I was wondering if anyone was sitting there." The man gestured to the chair Jennie had vacated.

"No, I mean yeah—I mean," He closed his eyes and took a breath, "I mean, my sister was sitting here, but she just went to say hi to some friends."

The man smiled and held out a hand, "I'm Adam."

"Mike." They shook. Adams hand was nice in

Mike's, smooth, masculine.

"Mind if I sit here for a bit?"

"No, not at all."

Adam sat down. He was not too tall and not overly muscular which was nice. His shirt was unbuttoned at the top and exposed just the right amount of mystery. Mike tried not to stare. For a moment he wondered if his harpy of an ex had figured everything out and was setting him up but no, it was far too late for her to get revenge that way.

See, once upon a time, in the long distant land of adolescence, Mike kissed a boy and liked it. Mike touched a boy and liked it. Mike tasted a boy and really, really liked it.

Mike also buried those desires and married the harpy in the hopes those urges—the ones he had always been told were wrong and of the devil—would go away. They didn't, of course. They tended to resurface every now and then, like now. Mike sipped his drink. Adam reminded him of Virgil. Virgil with his dark hair and deep dark eyes. Virgil who committed suicide because of the teasing from his classmates. Virgil who was Mike's first kiss. They had been what? Nine? Ten? No, eleven, that was it. He remembered they had been playing truth or dare, in the basement of his friend John's house.

****

John dared Mike to kiss Virgil. The girls laughed. Virgil looked terrified at first before feigning anger.

"That's gross John!" Virgil complained but his eyes didn't agree.

"Truth or dare. He chose dare." John shrugged, "That's the dare." The girls at the party tittered and hid behind hand covered smiles.

Virgil scowled. "Not where anyone can see."

"How are we supposed to know you actually do it?" One of the girls asked.

"I won't do it," Virgil protested.

"What are you? Chicken?" Teased John.

"Screw you." Virgil seemed on the edge of tears.

"Whatever," Mike was done with the stupidity of the game, "Let's just do it and get it over with."

"Ohh, Mikey wants it!" A brunette in pig tails spoke up. He thought her name might be Tiffany or Trixie or something stupid starting with a T.

Mike glared at her. "Shut up," he said, "It's a dare, that's all."

"Fine." Virgil gave in.

Mike had always liked Virgil. He was smart, creative, and full of funny stories. Mike thought of those things as he leaned across the circle and kissed Virgil, a quick peck on the lips, before leaning back and wiping his mouth off, while Virgil stuck his tongue out at John. It was not their last kiss.

A year later, Mike spent the night at Virgil's house. They watched movies and played video games until his mom came downstairs and told them it was time to go to sleep. Mike crawled into the bed next to Virgil. In the dark, they found themselves face to face. Mike didn't speak. Neither did Virgil, but both were acutely aware of each other. It was Mike who made the first move and reached a tentative, shaky hand across to touch the lock of hair hanging in front of Virgil's face.

Virgil reached up and took his hand. "Do you remember…" his voice trailed off.

Mike nodded and they kissed again.

This time, with nothing but the dark, the blankets, the silent witness of the moon above them, they kissed longer, opening their mouths, and letting their tongues explore each other. Mike was suddenly hard. Surprised he started to pull back, but Virgil reached down and wrapped a hand around Mike's erection.

"It's okay," Virgil whispered and guided Mike's free hand to his own, "Just move your hand up and down and squeeze as you go up." Mike shut his brain off to any questions or objections and let the forbidden desires take over. He let his imagination go with it. After all, it was Virgil, his friend, the boy next door.

Their friendship deepened, and they started spending more time with each other. At school they tried their hardest to blend in and not get picked on. They were both slight, small, and more on the scholarly side rather than the jock side of life. Mike had a hard enough time at home with his military father pushing him to be what he wasn't. Virgil was a welcome spirit: someone he could relate to. Their innocent explorations were just that, innocent and beautifully pure. They were careful not to draw attention to themselves in public.

Mike didn't think anything weird about their friendship until one of the bullies called him a sissy and asked if Virgil was his girlfriend. It was after a football game, their freshman year in high school. The jock caught them leaning close, talking, and laughing under the bleachers.

"I always knew you were a faggot." He pointed a finger at Mike. "Does your dad know about your girlfriend here?"

Virgil glared at him. "I'm not his girlfriend."

"Oh yeah?" The bully challenged, "Then he must be

yours."

"Shove off." Mike's fists clenched.

"Or what?" The bully asked, "You going to tattle on me? Cause if you do, I will happily tell your dad you were sucking Virgil here off."

"Like he would believe you," Virgil replied.

But Mike was scared. His dad was retired Military and already thought Mike was a pansy. "Fuck you," he said but lacked conviction.

The bully laughed and walked off with his friends. "I'm watching you," he warned.

Had someone been watching? Could they tell what Mike and Virgil had been up to? Fear washed through Mike. His dad would kill him. He felt himself go cold, his mouth dry up, his spirit wilt.

"We should avoid each other for a while," he whispered, leaving Virgil standing alone as Mike walked away.

The following Monday at school Mike was embarrassed and torn as to what to do. He didn't think he was gay. He was far too young to know, right? His parents and his preacher all said being gay was a sin, but he liked Virgil. He thought what they were doing was beautiful and right. It felt right. It felt better than the one time he kissed a girl. Still the words of his elders rang in his ears and when he passed Virgil in the hallway at school, he looked the other way, and ignored his friend.

Two weeks later, Virgil hung himself from the rafters of his garage. Mike blamed himself. He should have never ignored his friend. He should have said something. He buried his guilt and desires in school, throwing himself into his classes so he wouldn't have to think.

It was a pattern he would repeat for years.

****

The first year in college, before Mike met his soon to be wife, he went to a drag show with some friends. A tall, dark haired, mahogany skinned goddess of a drag Queen wearing a short, red dress with long legs in high platform red pumps, lips painted red, vibrant red was performing. Watching the way her boy body moved awoke something in him.

Mike leaned in closer, hypnotized as she ran a hand down her short sequined dress, shimmying her hips, licking her red painted lips and suddenly he had a raging hard on. He staggered to the bathroom, doing his best to walk without giving away his bulging erection. The only thing he could do was relieve himself. Unzipping his fly, Mike took his dick in his hands. He was in the middle of stroking himself off when the door opened.

It was the drag queen.

Mike burned with embarrassment. She took one look at Mike, assessed the situation, and said, "Oh honey, let me take care of that."

Mike hadn't known what to say, but just the thought of those red painted lips on his cock made him nod his head.

She locked the door and knelt before him taking his cock in her mouth, swallowing him whole and milking his shaft. She held his balls in her strong hands while she worked her mouth up and down, up, and down, teasing him, tasting him, licking his shaft, nibbling ever so slightly. And those red painted lips...it was the best blow job Mike ever experienced.

When he came in her mouth she leaned back, licked her lips, stood up and held out her hand. "Wow, you just made my night honey," she said, "I'm Karina Fire."

"Karina?"

"Well…" she gestured at her outfit, "Right now I am Karina but later when I change, I will be Thomas."

"Thomas."

"You're new here, aren't you?"

"You could say that," he found his voice. "It's nice to meet you and uh thank you."

"My pleasure baby. My pleasure." She moved to the mirror and adjusted her wig, "I always like a little treat after a performance." Looking pointedly at his cock Karina added, "Not that you are anywhere near the definition of little."

Mike didn't know what to do. Did he pay her? Was she like a prostitute? Was he expected to return the favor?

He watched her in the mirror for a moment before turning her around to kiss. She may have been dressed like a woman but underneath the make-up and red sequined short dress she was all male. She turned down his offer of a hand job saying she needed to perform again, slipped him her number, and asked him to meet her after she finished for the night.

He left the bathroom and returned to his friends. They went home laughing and teasing each other along the way, swearing they were too macho to fall for a man in women's clothing. Mike laughed with them but once they got back to the dorm he slipped out and went back.

Thomas was waiting for him, dressed in jeans, loafers, and a white shirt. Mike did not consider himself brave, but his attraction to Thomas dressed as Karina was intense. Mike had never been so turned on as when he reached a hand between Karina's legs earlier in the tight little dress and found his cock tucked safely away.

The guilt came back the next day when his friends started verbally bashing gays and their lifestyle. He didn't want to be hated or ostracized or end up a victim. In the end, Mike ignored his urges, denied his desire, and buried himself in school.

He met his harpy of an ex shortly after that night. Her lips were painted red and she was wearing a red dress when he saw her. She was tall, slim, with short dark hair and a commanding presence. The red immediately reminded him of the drag Queen Karina; Mike wanted to kiss her. The red dress and dark hair were the only things the harpy had in common with Karina Fire. The harpy was cold, domineering, and condescending whereas Karina, in the short brief time Mike knew her, seemed fun, flirtatious, and full of spirit.

The harpy roped Mike in, put him on a leash and controlled his life. Once they got together, Mike did his best to deny himself what he genuinely wanted and pretend to be in love with the harpy.

****

Now looking at Adam, Mike wondered just what would have been different if his secret feelings, and strong attraction to men, had not always been pushed aside?

"Do you come here often?" Adam asked. "Sorry, that was very cliché."

"It's okay," Mike relaxed and let out a small laugh, "I'm usually only here on the weekends, in the morning. You?"

"Came to hear the bands. I know the drummer in Void."

"Is that who's playing now?"

"No, this is Monkeys Breath. Void is next."

"Nice." Mike nodded. He didn't know what to say. He wanted to keep Adam talking so he could watch those lips move. "Are you from here?"

"Right now." Adam gave Mike a nice let me undress you smile. "I have traveled a lot. Military brat." As if that explained everything. "You?"

"I grew up in Everett. Lived in Redmond for a while and just moved here to Seattle about six months ago."

"Do you like it?"

Mike shrugged. "It's nice. There is a lot to do."

Adam leaned in a bit closer. "Do you go out a lot?"

Mike studied the intricate woodwork of the bar, the dark and light polished grains. "To be honest, this is the first time I have gone out."

"Lucky me." Adam licked his lips.

Mikes heart started dancing. The way Adam was checking him out felt like an invitation, or a dare to see what Mike would do. He felt the desires kick in. He looked at Adam's lips and wondered what they would feel like, what he would look like with his shirt off. Was he smooth? Did he have fine hair?

Mike took another sip of his drink and looked away. Jennie. Jennie was out on the dance floor. She was with her friends. He needed to think of Jennie. What would she do if she saw him kiss a man?

Adam backed off a bit, "Have I read you wrong? If you aren't into men, I apologize."

"No," Mike fumbled with the words, "You're right. It's just been a while since I have done the casual hook up scene."

Adam laughed, "How long?"

"Too long." Mike replied, "I'm still not out." He

sounded lame. Here he was thirty years old and not out? A closeted middle-aged man? How stupid did that sound? Like something out of the nineteen fifties. Like someone who was afraid to be who he was. "My divorce was just finalized six months ago." He didn't know why he felt the need to explain things to this stranger, "I'm still working on getting myself back together. I spent so many years sneaking around."

"All those clandestine moments hooking up in the back alleys, parked cars, and bathrooms." Adam smiled knowingly.

"Or parks," Mike said, mouth dry.

"You want another?" Adam pointed to his empty glass.

"Not yet, uhm…" Mike stood up, "bathroom… would you excuse me?"

"You want some company?"

Mikes palms started to sweat. He did, but he didn't, but he did. "What if someone is in there?"

"Then nothing happens." Adam shrugged.

"It's been a while…"

"It's like riding a bike." Adam reached out, took Mike's hand, and traced his fingers.

It was like a slow electrical pulse spreading through his body. Mike wanted to lean in, pull Adam close, taste his luscious lips, but restrained himself. There were people around who might recognize him from earlier, like the mystery writer who still sat at the end of the table watching and taking notes. Or the skinny waitress with the shaved head who had been helping the barista/guitar player out in the morning. He didn't know if any of them knew who he was, but he didn't want them putting two and two together with his little escapades.

He managed a smile at Adam before retreating to the bathroom. The hallway was dark, and he narrowly missed bumping into a blonde woman and her Latino lover. They pretty much oozed sex which did not help Mike out. He could smell it coming off them like the sweet scent of cinnamon.

He staggered past them and stepped into the bathroom. His cock strained against his zipper, and he willed it to go down. He thought of his ex, which usually helped, but this time her image kept getting replaced by the thought of Adam's lips, of Thomas's lips, of red painted lips on his cock. Mike groaned and stepped into a stall, leaning against the wall. He heard the door open and the lock slide shut. His breath started to come in short gasps. He heard footsteps stop outside the stall he was in, followed by a short knock.

"Open the door."

It was Adam.

Mike froze. He couldn't do it. He wouldn't do it. The guilt—the fear of being found out, all those years spent in denial. "No." He barely recognized the croak of his voice.

"It's okay," Adam whispered from the other side. "I understand."

Mike closed his eyes. He wasn't used to this blatant attraction, it scared him, tipped the scales of his world. To think he could be in a room and people could see his truth, recognize it. He was so used to hiding who he was, so used to his secret moments of satisfaction.

"Don't deny yourself your truth," Adam challenged.

"I'm not," Mike insisted. He closed his eyes and leaned against the door. He was still hard. His penis felt like it was going to burst through his pants. It was the sound of Adam's voice, the smell of him like the two lovers he passed in the hallway, cinnamon. Mike took a deep breath and willed his heart to calm down.

"Mike." Adams voice carried a sliver of suggestion, "Open the door."

"No, please go away."

"No."

Mike started to shake. He wanted to touch Adam, undress him, unzip his pants, and free his cock. To swallow him.

Adam said nothing but Mike sensed movement on the other side of the door. He wasn't sure what was going on until suddenly Adam's red and black shirt slipped ghostlike across the top. It puddled at Mike's feet.

He reached down, picked it up, and smelled it, burying his nose in the scent of cinnamon, wood, and musk. Unbidden Mike opened the door, and stared into Adam's dark eyes, took in his naked chest, the faint wispy trail of dark curls leading down past the belt, past the buckle, past the zipper and oh how Mike wanted to unzip those pants. He licked his lips.

"I think it's time you came out of the closet," Adam whispered.

He was right. It was an attraction, it was sex, and what was it they said? Ninety percent of the population was truly bi-sexual. Something like that? Mike didn't know what was true or what wasn't. He knew he was unsure. He knew he was attracted to men. He knew he was attracted to red lips. He knew he liked men in red dresses. He just had no idea why or what it all meant. He also knew he didn't want to delve too deeply into his subconscious to find out.

"It's just sex," Adam said and moved closer, inches

away, "Just pure, hot, sex."

Mike could feel the heat pulsing off Adam, could feel his desire growing. He stared into Adam's eyes and gave in, kissing him, letting his hands rove across Adam's chest, feeling the hardness of his muscles, the faint beat of his heart and as Mike slipped a hand down he felt the promise of Adam's cock.

Mike groaned.

"What do you want?" Adam pulled his head back, gazing at Mike from half lidded eyes.

"You." Mike pressed him against the stall, devouring him, drowning in him, his body, his taste, his scent. It was pure heat, a slow burning field of lava that could not be quenched. Adams lips on his, his tongue in Mike's mouth, Adam's fingers in Mike's hair, on his chest, wrapped around his cock and then Adam's hot mouth melting around Mike as he took Mike inside.

She ate the banana...

He stroked his penis...

Red lips on firm flesh, mouth working up and down his shaft, tongue wrapping around, teeth nibbling. Mike was a mix of emotions, of sensations, of pleasure. Everything zeroed into the hunger, the need for release, and Mike let himself experience it all, feel it. He dug his fingers into the soft dark curls of Adam's hair, pumped himself into Adam's moist, warm mouth, and when Adam cupped his balls, Mike cried out.

Red tipped fingernails tickled his balls...

Red lips worked up and down his shaft...

Red...only they were no longer red. It was Adams lips, Virgil's lips, a man's lips on his cock, taking him in, draining him...

And he came, all the pent-up denial, all the emotions

locked away, his past his present, all collided, erupted and his world spun, out of focus, out of control. He lost his bearing's, his balance, his heart was racing, pounding, breath coming in short quick gasps.

Adam stood up, licked his lips, and grinned at Mike. "It's not a bad thing." Adam said, and Mike had to laugh.

"Hello!" There was a knock at the door, "Other people need to use the bathroom you know?"

Mike started at the sound. "Shit," he whispered. The fears and doubts crashed back into place.

Adam buttoned his shirt and tucked it into his pants. "It's okay." He said quickly glancing up, "We were talking business."

"Business." Mike was still reeling, off balance mentally and drained physically.

"Yes. Business." Adam reached over and helped Mike get dressed. "We were discussing stocks and what to invest in and we didn't want to be disturbed so we locked the door. Now pull yourself together Mike."

"Okay." Mike nodded. Business. They locked the door because they were discussing things. It was a cover. It could work. "Won't it look like we were just doing drugs or something?"

"Possibly." Adam grinned, moved over to the sink, washed his hands, and wet his hair.

"Come on," the voice on the other side pleaded.

"Sorry," Mike answered, "Just a minute." He straightened his shirt a bit and checked himself out in the mirror. Deep breaths, he told himself, deep breaths.

"I'm going to unlock it." Adam reached for the lock.

"Wait." Mike held up a hand.

"Yes?" Adam turned towards him.

Mike drew in another breath. He let it fill him, let it

tamper down the confusion, the fear, and the past. He rotated his shoulders and walked over to Adam, two short steps, face to face again but this time…this time Mike was not scared.

"One for the road." Kissing Adam quick before Mike could change his mind. He reached behind Adam and unlocked the door. They broke apart.

"Sorry about that." Mike said, mask in place, "We had some business to discuss."

"Isn't that what office hours are for?" The man glared and moved past them.

Mike didn't respond. He reached behind him for Adams hand and pulled him next to him, "Thank you." He whispered, letting go as they entered the main room.

The owner of Secrets, Eli, was on stage. He announced the band "Void" and stepped down. The lights flashed red, then yellow, before fading into red again. Mike and Adam made their way back to the bar. The couple from earlier were standing draped in each other's arms, leaning over the area where Mike and Adam had left their coats. The scent of sex wafted off the couple like smoke from a still smoldering fire.

Mike didn't have the heart to ask them to move. He gathered up his long wool coat, once again wishing he'd left it in the car, and handed Adam his leather jacket.

"Thank you. You ready for another drink?" Adam asked.

"Sure," Mike replied.

Adam slipped into his leather coat and they got in line. Mike looked around for Jennie. She was still talking to her friends. He managed to catch her eye to see if she was okay. She gave him a thumbs up.

The uncomfortable what do I say to the guy who just

got me off silence descended upon him. He was at a loss as to what to do next. This had happened before. He felt like he should have reciprocated. But when? It wasn't like Mike could take Adam back to his place. Not with Jennie staying there. Besides, they'd just met. Were they supposed to date? What did someone do when they came out of the closet?

He risked a glance at Adam. God, he was sexy, dark, mysterious, lean, and those lips, that ass. It had been a while since Mike allowed himself the luxury of enjoying sex with a man. What if he was bad? What if he couldn't do it? What if he sucked and not in a good way?

"So, where do you work?"

Small talk, what a relief. "I work as a computer analysis."

"Really?"

"We mostly investigate company profiles and make sure there aren't any issues, and that they are protected. What do you do?"

"I oversee product control for a couple of the stores at the University Village Shops."

"Gentlemen, what can I get for you?" The bartender asked as they made it to the front.

"I got this." Adam ordered the second round. They moved to the side and waited for their drinks.

"Where do you normally sit when you come here?" Adam scanned the crowded room.

"Outside."

"Outside?"

"Yes. There is a little seating area, but I think it's closed at night." Mike glanced over towards the doors. He could just make out some string lights. "Maybe."

"Let's check it out." Adam followed his gaze.

They wove their way through the throngs of people. Mike led the way. He stopped at the door, pausing just a second when his eyes caught on a woman with red painted lips who looked strikingly like the woman from earlier. But no, it couldn't be…could it? She disappeared in the masses, and he shook it off.

He pushed at the door and was surprised when it swung open. In the background a cheer went up as Void finished their first song. Mike and Adam stepped out into the empty seating space. At night there was a magical quality to it. The potted plants at the corners gave it a more secluded look. The string lights hanging overhead cast a soft glow to the area. It was like a small oasis. Even the sounds of the city seemed distant.

Adam looked around and nodded his approval. "Nice."

"It is." Mike agreed. They couldn't be seen from inside or the street. It was more isolated and stimulating at night then during the day. He looked around the area, checking it out and the possibilities…he rubbed at his crotch, feeling himself harden.

"Wow, it is really private out here." Adam walked in a small circle, taking it in.

"It is," Mike replied. He spied the table the red lipped woman sat at earlier in the morning. It was in the shadows, obscured. He looked over at Adam, resplendent in his dark clothing: leather jacket, shirt unbuttoned and pants tight against his lean form. His hair was gently traced by moonlight. Mike bit his lip. He knew what he wanted. He just hoped he could do it.

"Come here." He took Adams hand, led him to the table and sat him down. Mike removed his long wool coat, folded it in half and knelt on it. His heart was beating. His tongue was dry. He took a sip of his drink, stared into Adam's dark night shade eyes and with slightly shaky hands undid his zipper.

"You sure?" Adam asked.

"Yes, please." Mike wanted to taste it. He took Adams cock in his hands. It was hard, smooth, and warm. He ran his tongue up and down the shaft, getting it wet, lubricating it.

She ate the banana...

He stroked his penis...

Mike moved his hand up and down Adams cock, squeezing slightly as he went up and released the pressure as he went down. He did what he liked done on himself. He opened his mouth and slipped Adams cock inside. It filled him, and he gagged as it hit the back of his throat, bringing water to his eyes.

"Yes, yes," Adam moaned.

Mike pulled back and shook his head, took a deep breath and did it again making sure to keep his teeth from rubbing against the skin. He used his tongue to lick and curl around the shaft and alternated going up then down with his mouth working Adam's penis in, then out. He cupped the balls, squeezing them gently and licking at them before releasing them and playing with the penis. It felt alive in his mouth, and he listened for Adam's reactions, the soft moans, feeling Adam dig his fingers into Mike's hair, hold him down and whisper "Yes, yes, right there."

Mike kept doing what he was doing, tried reciprocate the moves, the licking, the sucking, the up and down motion.

"Faster, please, yes" Adam begged, and Mike obliged. He bobbed his head up and down, sucking harder, going deeper, taking the shaft in until he almost heaved. Then back out, up, down, alternating nibbles with licks, faster, faster, faster. He felt tears wet the edges of his eyes, but he didn't care, what mattered was the sounds Adam was making, the way his hips suddenly started to move, the urgency of his hands in Mike's hair and the soft cries. Mike kept going, tasting the precum, the slight salty caramel flavor of it.

"Oh yes! God! Yes! Don't stop! That's it!" Adam pumped his penis in and out and held onto Mike as if he was drowning. Adam's dick spasmed, quick jerks and suddenly, he was coming, exploding in convulsive waves.

Mike swallowed and kept it down.

"Stop. Shit, stop," Adam gasped and Mike leaned back.

He wiped a drop of cum from his mouth. "Was that, okay?"

"Okay?" Adam laughed, "Shit, Mike. That was—oh my God—fantastic."

Mike smiled. Something inside him shifted, like it was opening a door and seeing freedom on the other side, as if it had been trapped behind glass walls for too long and just needed to break free. He reached for his drink, took a long swallow, and stood up.

"You need to come out." Adam laughed, running a hand through his dark hair, "I mean, why hide? You are…wow."

"Thank you." Mike ducked his head so Adam wouldn't see him blushing. "We should get back inside."

"We should, just give me a minute to get my feet back under me," Adam said, "You kind of knocked me for a loop there."

Mike didn't know what to say. He did feel strangely satisfied with himself. Stretching, he glanced around at the night clad area and tattooed it into his memory. This would be a fantasy he would pull up again and again. *Like the red lips*...whispered his subconscious and he shook his head.

"Wow," Adam repeated, "You were great."

Mike took his hand and pulled Adam to him. "Thank you." Mike kissed him.

"You still taste like me," Adam said.

"Then we are equal," Mike replied, "Because you taste like me."

They kissed again, long, and deep, tongues probing, tasting and it felt right, normal. Mike's emotions were swirling about him. He wanted to walk inside holding Adams hand, but what would Jennie think if she saw? What if someone from his job saw him? He needed to deal with those fears. They broke apart. Mike picked up his coat, shook it out. They went back inside.

He let his eyes adjust and searched for his sister. She was on the dance floor. The band was playing a song with a chorus that seemed to scream at his subconscious "Just do it do it do it and be free!"

"Let me give you, my number," Adam said, "We could get together again."

Mike looked into Adams deep dark eyes and wanted to do it again. If he came out of the closet, it could be like this. He wouldn't be nervous, or hesitant, he could just be who he was and no longer have to hide.

But could he?

"I...uhm..." He hesitated.

"I didn't come out until I was twenty-five," Adam admitted.

"What happened?"

"Nothing." Adam laughed, his eyes crinkling at the corners. "Once I said the words, I was free."

"But what about your family? Your job?"

"They didn't care." Adam sipped his drink, "You would be amazed at the weight it lifts off your shoulders."

"But—"

"What?" Adam held his gaze, "Let go of your fears Mike."

"What if these…these cravings…these thoughts aren't—"

"Aren't what? Really who you are?" Adam put his hand on his shoulder, "Mike, these urges you have, these desires, they are real. They are okay. You have this secret buried inside you and it's been trying to get out for years. And yet, you are too afraid of what people might think to let it out. Let it out Mike, let yourself be happy." Adam leaned in close, "Trust me Mike, I understand. Pretty much every gay man who has come out later in life understands what you are going through."

"But—"

"No buts Mike, the harsh reality is this, you can deny yourself your truth and be miserable and lost or, you can stand up and be who you are. Sometimes the hardest thing to say is, I'm gay. But when you do, it will release you." He held a business card out.

Mike stared into the truth of Adam's eyes, nodded, took the card, and tucked it into his pocket. He took out his wallet, tugging free his own business card. Mike didn't see a second business card float to the floor.

"You're right." He admitted and handed it to Adam, "I need to do it. Not tonight though."

"Call me when you do," Adam said.

"I will." There was so much more he wanted to say, words he should say, but he couldn't. He looked over at his sister talking to her friends. She looked so fragile suddenly, so hurt, like a bird that had just lost the ability to fly. She caught his eyes and he saw the breakdown, saw the melting of her heart, and heard the cries of her soul.

"Shit."

"What?" Adam followed his gaze.

"My sister." Mike hastily explained, "She just got into town today and she's fragile. It's too complicated to explain right now, but I have to go. She needs me." He reached for Adams hand and squeezed it, "Thank you." He whispered in Adam's ear before hurrying over to her.

Mike didn't look back to see if Adam was watching. Mike didn't look back to see if he upset Adam. He didn't see Adam tuck the card away and turn towards the door. He didn't see the dark-haired woman with the red painted lips swoop down and grab the second business card from the floor. He didn't see her look over his way in triumph and take the card. All he saw was his sister and the pain suddenly etched on her face.

"Jennie, are you okay?"

She was on the verge of tears. The unspoken communication between siblings spilled the truth and he suddenly understood.

"Was that him?" Mike asked, and she nodded. The whole story sank in. The guitar player, the barista, Todd, was the father of the unborn child.

He wrapped his sister in his arms and held her. He saw Todd talking to the waitress with the buzz cut from earlier. Mike looked for Adam but didn't see him anywhere. He tilted his sister's face up. "Want to go home?" He asked and she nodded.

She needed him.

She leaned on him as they stepped out into the embrace of the night. The lights of the city hovered above them like ghosts. He rounded the corner and headed towards the parking garage. He vaguely heard someone calling out her name in the background but Jennie was crying. He got her into his car and drove them the short distance to his apartment. They hit every red light on the way. Mike wondered if it was a sign of how his life had been derailed for years by red lights, people telling him who he needed to be, and his own burial of the truth. Would he ever have the strength to let himself be who he was? It was a secret he needed to let out.

He looked over at his sister huddled into herself, crying over a past she couldn't fix. He didn't want to burden her with his confession right now. Tonight, his sister needed her brother.

Chapter 12

Shh…Don't Answer?

It was almost noon when I stopped writing. Flexing my fingers, a quick glance at my phone let me know I had fifteen minutes to get to work. I finished my coffee, stuffed my notebook in my bag, and rushed to the door. I bumped into a blonde woman wearing a long white coat over a red top and gray skirt. She was the kind of woman you couldn't help noticing, blonde bob, ice blue eyes, and well dressed. Mumbling an apology, I hurried past her and made it to work where I spent the rest of the day dealing with one mess after another. The only thing that got me through my shift was the thought of some whiskey. I could hardly wait to return to Secret's Café.

The music greeted me as I came around the corner that evening. I'd forgotten it was the battle of the bands. A cluster of people hung outside the entrance, talking and smoking. The sweet scent of marijuana drifted in the air, and I sniffed, savoring it. Passing the alley, I saw a few of the city's homeless setting up camp. Seattle was a different lover at night, she did her best, but her walls couldn't warm the down and out.

I felt the skin on the back of my neck prickle like someone was watching me or walking over my future grave. There were a lot of people around. It could have been anyone. Glancing around, seeing no one, I shrugged the feeling off and pushed the door open. The music surged past me like a wave crashing into shore.

It was packed. I got in line for a drink. A honey haired twenty something got in line behind me. We waited for the two bartenders to work their magic, move the line forward, and provide us with the sustenance we needed, wanted.

The band was rather good. There was a distinctive sound to the music, a kind of poetry, wistful and heart tugging. The lead singer's voice was smoky and the lyrics like a story. I found myself moving to the beat, tapping my foot. I was used to dancing alone but this sound made me want to be out on the floor. Maybe after a drink.

I felt a tingle on my skin again, like someone's eyes were walking over my body, and glanced over my shoulder. My phone vibrated in my pocket. I took it out hoping it was Thomas. The woman behind me took hers out as well. Together we swiped the screens to life. Synchronicity.

It was Secret, the twenty-year-old mistake I was trying to close the book on. My heart surged for a beat or two before tucking tail and hiding.

Her message read:

—This is getting old. Neither of you are talking to me—

I arched an eyebrow at her words, saved it to her creepy file, and put my phone back at the same time as the brunette behind me. The messages *were* getting old. They had started off whiney and moved into the freaky zone. I had erased the first few but was now saving them just in case she went bat shit crazy and tried to do anything.

The band announced their last song. I took a step up in the line and vowed not to think about the mistake. Instead, I mulled over how I could use the scene in my story idea. How would I describe it? *The red lights and the way the crowd was silhouetted in shapes moving like a red ocean; the band stood out, etched in flickering red; the drummer ready to go, the lead singer with his head down counting, gripping the microphone, looking to the guitar player to start before staring out into the sea of faces and*…I stopped, focusing on the lead singer. It was Todd, the barista. Wow, color me surprised. Todd was a man with hidden talents.

"What can I get for you tonight?" Jay, the bartender snagged my focus.

"Godfather with a whiskey back." It was a sweet cocktail, but the extra shot could take it down a notch.

Elan, the waitress from earlier, joined the honey haired woman behind me. She slipped an arm around her and nuzzled into the woman's neck. Love and romance oozed from them like sticky melted chocolate. I was slightly jealous and yet happy for Elan. She looked like life had been mean to her. I paid for my drink and found a seat at the bar not too far from the line.

Draping my coat over the back of the chair, I took my notebook out and started to write the scene down: the way the sound of the crowd overlapped in conversations so one couldn't follow it; the way one simply caught threads here and there, but they were like beads waiting to be connected from different strings; how the red lights played on people's faces casting a different kind of glow. Glow. I needed a different word. Luminous? Light? Reflect? No, those wouldn't work, there had to be something more poetic, more powerful. What was it with the red lights anyway? Didn't exotic dancers perform under red lights? I took my phone out to search red lights and another message popped up. Fucking Secret, give it a rest.

—God, Georgia, how pathetic you are, sitting by yourself focused on your notebook. I don't know what I ever saw in you—

How did she know I was alone with my notebook out? I picked up my drink, casually sipped it, set the phone down, and let my eyes rove about the bar. She had to be somewhere nearby, but where? What the hell was her game?

Elan and the honey haired girl stood behind me. Todd's band finished playing. The crowd cheered, clapped, and the lights brightened a notch. There were too many people in the room. Too many places she could be hiding. Too many shadows able to absorb her. I should finish my drink and leave but wouldn't I be letting her win? Wasn't that what she wanted? To see me run and hide? It was all empty threats anyway. But what if it wasn't? What if she tried something? In a room full of people? The questions circled like vultures waiting for me to panic. I closed my eyes and centered myself.

"How are we doing here?" The bartender checked on me. I ordered another, minus the second shot. He brought it over and set it down. I finished the first one, feeling the smooth mix relax me.

Todd joined the lovebirds behind me, and I went back to the page. My main character was trying to get away from his evil, manipulative ex by going to a Christmas party, where he would meet someone new, someone who would come off as intriguing but who would end up being hired by his ex to drive him crazy, to ruin his life. I had left off where the woman agreed to meet him the next day at a breakfast place and show him what she could do with a banana. I read over what I'd written, crossed a few things off, and was just about to put pen to paper when the lights flashed, dimmed to red, and Eli announced the next band, Void.

I waited, letting my eyes adjust. The band started with a ballad. It was haunting and perfect background noise. I turned to the page and started to write.

She sat down across from him like he had asked and slowly peeled the banana. He moved the newspaper to his lap and undid his pants, glancing quickly around to see if he could be seen. She smiled at him and licked her lips, poised them over the phallic flesh—

My phone flashed and I picked it up reluctantly, not sure if I even wanted to check it. Cautiously I clicked on it and was only slightly relieved to see it was a message from Diana.

—*Hey darling!*—Darling? Yuck.—*Hope your day went well. Want me to pick you up Saturday?*—

I was going to her place for dinner. I didn't have a car, but I also didn't want to be without an escape. I replied:

—*Thanks, but I'll take an uber. Do you need me to bring anything?*—

Diana—*Just your beautiful self.*—

Me—*I'll see if I can dig the beautiful part out. Ha! Ha*—

Diana—*Ha! Ha! You're gorgeous*—Followed by a kissy face emoji and one with stars in its eyes.

God, were we in elementary school again? I shuddered.

Me:—*I'll bring some wine. See you tomorrow*—

Diana and I were practically the same age: we had things in common, could carry on a conversation, and it was nice to have a woman friend. Janet and Lori were good friends, but when I was around them, I felt like a third wheel invited out of pity. Most of my friends ended up cutting me off after Leslie died. They blamed me for not being there. I could have been upset about that, but they had been her friends from the start and mine after the fact. It was so hard to come by real friends. The question with Diana was, did I like her as more than a friend? The answer was no. I enjoyed her company but did not see myself growing old with her and living with her. Hell, I didn't see myself growing old with anyone at this point in my life. I needed to figure me out first before venturing into relationship land.

Thomas had nailed it when he said I picked the wrong people. I did. I didn't know if I picked them on purpose or if the universe was trying to teach me a lesson. I didn't even know what the lesson was. Maybe I just needed to learn to love myself, to live on my own? Relationships didn't define who I was. Being a partner, another half didn't define me anymore than who I chose to have sex with, what profession I chose or what religion I picked to follow. Everyone was a puzzle and personally I thought everyone hid something, some part of themselves behind a mask. A truth or fear they don't want known.

Oh! I could use that. I cocked my head to the side and the idea circled like smoke. The personal demons people hid behind masks, like the fear of coming out and not being accepted. Or the fear of not being good enough, of not measuring up to someone's expectations! Or the perfection issue! Where one has a list and she or he thought it's what he or she wanted but it wasn't! And my personal favorite, the trust issue, where a person has been broken and needs to learn to trust. I could give each of my characters something to hide, a mask they would need to shed. This would add some depth. I liked it. I scribbled the idea down on the empty page and circled it.

Todd suddenly bumped me, clutching at the bar. I moved my notebook out of reach for fear of alcohol spilling on it, destroying the words, smudging them into non-existence.

"Jay," Elan leaned over me, and waved at the bartender, "Another rum and coke for Todd."

"No, make it a whiskey," Todd said, and his voice cracked, breaking over the words,. "A double."

"Double whiskey," Elan repeated to Jay.

I had missed something. Todd's eyes were wide, his face was white, and he looked like he'd been hit by a brick wall. Elan placed a hand on his shoulder, with her other she reached for the drink Jay set down. Todd took the whiskey from her and slammed it. His eyes were far away, they were swirling in a vortex of pain. I followed his gaze to a woman in white. The lights danced about her, igniting her like she was an angel, a ghost. She was clearly someone who had just torn his world apart. I felt for him. I ached for him. My heart recognized the broken parts of him. I wanted to reach for him but didn't know him that well. Instead, I asked for the bill, finished my drink, and stood up. Jay handed over my tab and I dug out my wallet. My phone flashed with another message.

—*Slinking away so soon?*—

Secret. God, I hated her.

I scanned the people nearby but didn't see her. A woman at the end of the bar looked familiar except she was a messy haired blonde with lipstick smeared and eyes half closed. It wasn't until she lifted her chin that I recognized her as the fierce blonde I'd ran into when I left Secrets Café earlier. Damn. She looked a lot looser now, like she had devoured a five-course meal and watching the man next to her drink her in I was pretty sure I knew what she'd been dining on. Our eyes met and I gave her the briefest of nods. I recognized her drug. I used it myself.

I put my phone in my pocket, tucked my notebook away. Slipping my coat on, I wove through the crowd, checking to see if anyone was following me. I couldn't tell. Stepping into the cold bite of the night was like an electric shock. Winter was chomping at fall, wanting to take over. I burrowed myself in my coat and hurried for home, crossing First Avenue, and stopping outside of Vons to glance over my shoulder. I didn't see anyone.

****

Saturday evening, I took an uber to Diana's and thought twice about leaving when I arrived. It was too perfect of a set up. I felt like the fly invited into the spider's web. It took a lot of strength to get out of the car, walk up the short walkway, and knock on the front door.

Diana rented a small Craftsman style bungalow in the U District. It was my dream house, slate blue with white trim, two stained glass outlined windows, a deep mahogany wood door, and a couple of wicker chairs in one corner with a small table. A homespun rag rug lay in front of the door. Part of me wanted to move in, the other part said "Run for the hills! It's a trap!" I knocked.

Diana answered wearing jeans and a flannel shirt, and gave me a hug, ushering me in.

"Nice place." I slipped my jacket off and took in the

wood floors polished and scarred with stories, the fireplace flanked by bookshelves, and the rag rugs warming the feet of the furniture.

"Thank you, I like it." She gave me a light kiss that turned into a longer one, "Mumm," She nuzzled my ear, "I'd better stop before the food burns."

"Smells good," I said, "What are you cooking?"

"Ratatouille," she replied, as she walked back into what I assumed was the kitchen.

Her place was sparsely furnished with a blue and white striped couch, an old trunk doubling as a coffee table with a candle flickering on it. The candle gave off the comforting scent of cinnamon apples. Next to it was an open book, like she'd been reading before I walked in. *Staged,* whispered my paranoid mind. The book was one of my favorites. Had I mentioned it to her? Was that why she was reading it? At least she liked to read. That was a bonus. The idiots I dated before her could barely turn a page.

"I see you are reading *Everything Beautiful Begin After*."

She appeared in the archway with two glasses of wine, "It's such a beautiful book, the way he writes…sheer poetry."

It was my exact feelings. Was she saying it deliberately? Idiot number two played that game. He had gone to one of my friends and found out all he could about me before setting his trap. Was Diana doing the same thing? Was this all a ploy to get me to like her more? Was it fake? Or was it just my imagination? I took the wine from her and sipped at it. It was a Pinot noir, also one of my favorites.

In the back of my mind an alarm went off and I

started wondering how I could get out of there. Not wanting to be rude, I vowed to stay for dinner and keep my guard up.

I followed her into the kitchen. A little table was set up with plates, napkins, and a salad. She motioned to one of the chairs and I sat down. She turned the oven off and took out some hot bread and the dripping with cheese Ratatouille. Yeah, I was definitely staying for dinner. We made small talk as we ate, comparing books, and prodding at each other's past but not going too deep. Helping her with dishes afterwards, I took her up on a second glass of wine and we moved back into the living room.

I was trying to figure out how I could gracefully make my escape when she started kissing me. I almost resisted but gave in. Diana knew how to kiss. She started off slow, her tongue and lips trailing up my neck, light nibbles on my earlobe, one hand in my hair tugging in just the right way, the other slipping under my shirt, my bra and finding my hardening nipples. She pushed me back on the couch and pulled my shirt off. She took her time exploring me with her fingers, her tongue and I wanted to run, but then again, who am I kidding? I'm not one to turn down a chance at a good orgasm and Diana was experienced, mature, not a man, and didn't need to be taught anything. I pushed all the doubts out of my mind and let her have her way with me. She undressed me, drizzled some wine on my pussy and flicked her tongue up and down like a cat drinking cream, tasting my juices before burying her face between my legs, making a humming noise against my clit.

"God, you taste good."

I felt a vibration as she slipped something inside me.

It was small, like one of those little bullet or egg-shaped things I'd seen in stores. She pulled it out and moved it around the edges of my clit, my pussy lips. It was attached to her finger. I had seen those things but never really tried them. I tangled my fingers in her hair and closed my eyes. My body tuned everything out but the feel of her lips, her tongue, her fingers, and the buzzing. She found my g-spot, the heart of pleasure.

"Oh wow." I groaned and waves road over me, my body quivered.

She kept the pressure up, letting it climb, build and then backing off. Catching my breath, I was just about to wonder if that was it when she started again, the circling of the fingers, the thrusting in and out, her hand pumping, the vibration riding my clit. Her fingers were inside me and I was right there, right on the edge. I was hovering, my body one nerve of sensation when she pulled out.

What the bleep? I bit my lip, felt the orgasm fade, and started to notice how uncomfortable the couch was, how there was something digging into my left hip, how it sagged too much under my back. She started licking me again, slowly, nuzzling my clit with her nose, her tongue, her thumb. My clit was angry about the two lost orgasms. It kept moving out from her touch. It was sore and not having it. She licked at it and slipped her fingers back inside me. I let her try again but this time, I wasn't in the mood. My body had been twice denied, it was not going to wait for a third. After fifteen minutes she leaned back and gave me a lopsided grin.

"Guess I should have gone with the other two."

She should have, but I wasn't going to guilt her. "My fault." I sat up and reached for my panties, "I had a really long day, and the dinner was so good. I'm just tired."

She pulled her shirt on. "Next time," she promised.

"Next time," I replied, thinking fat chance on that. We talked a bit more before I made my escape.

When I got home, the first thing I did was take a shower, letting the room steam up and the hot water flush my skin red. When I finished, I dried off and slipped into my flannel robe and cozy slippers. I wished I had a joint. It sounded so good. Instead, I reached for the bottle of apple whiskey, opened it, took a swallow, and hit play on a mix of my all-time favorite alternative bands.

Opening the sliding glass doors, I leaned against them letting the cold air in, feeling it cool my heated skin, wishing it could somehow take away the sadness threatening to press me down. My friend with benefits wanted more and I was not into her that way. I needed to break things off with Diana. She was another mistake. It was as simple as that.

Above me, the moon hung like a hook fishing for the reflection of the stars. The city was a landscape of boxed buildings, boxed windows, and boxed lights. I took another swallow of the whiskey before going back inside and picking up my phone from the kitchen counter to plug it in. There was a message from Diana:

—Thanks for coming over, sorry about the...well, you know. Let me make it up to you. What are you doing Saturday?—

Another message popped through:

—You're home late. Hope your date went well—

Secret. I almost dropped my phone on the counter. She was seriously creeping me out. I called Thomas, but he didn't answer. Saturday night, he was either still at a show or off with one of his many admirers. Knowing him, I didn't leave a message, and texted instead:

—Are you available tomorrow? Etta's? I'll buy. I'm off so we can meet anytime but brunch sounds good. They have the omelet you love and those bloody Mary's...Let me know if eleven works? I need to talk.—

It was close to Pikes, which meant I could shop for some fresh vegetables and seafood on my way home.

I went through the house locking everything, checking it twice,. I lived on the fifth floor. Like who was going to scale the walls and break in? Spider man? Seriously? She had me on edge. I tossed and turned all night.

****

Sunday, I dressed in jeans, a skull studded shirt, my favorite boots, and my long wool coat. Thomas had texted earlier; he was down with eleven. Taking the elevator to the lobby, I paused at the entry way and checked outside for anyone loitering nearby. This was what my life had become. I hated her for it.

After gathering my courage, holding my head high, I pushed the door open and stepped out into winters grasp. The weather was breezy. Leaves were clinging desperately to the trees only to be torn asunder and sent floundering into the sky. My long coat whipped about my feet and I wished for a hat, earmuffs, scarf, anything to keep my ears warm. Regret. Shit. The breeze bit at my eyes and I was grateful for wearing glasses but still, I couldn't focus on the people around me. She could have been standing next to me dressed in a scarf and I would have been clueless.

I fought my way to Pikes Place, ducked into the stalls, and savored the protection. Sundays were slower at the market. Catching my breath, I stood for a moment before walking past the vendors to price check items for later. Meandering through the fruit, vegetable, and seafood stands was a favorite part of my days off. There were so many choices, so many unique items only available in Seattle, it was hard to pick just one. The creativity of mealtimes had become a favorite hobby to me.

Etta's was past the market and across the street from the Victor Steinbrueck Park. I pushed the door open, fighting with the wind a bit, and staggered inside. Shaking my hair and rubbing my hands together for warmth, I took in the different, unique stained-glass lamps hanging above the dining area. The hostess greeted me and led me to a small table.

Thomas arrived, dressed in jeans, a long red cloak, and a fedora with a feather struggling to stay clasped to the brim. He removed the sunglasses he didn't need to be wearing, sighted me, and nodded to the hostess, who did all but hold out a menu for his autograph.

"You look like shit," he said as he sat down.

"Wow, thank you," I drizzled the phrase with as much sarcasm as I could muster.

Thomas arched a perfectly manicured eyebrow at me. "Darling, if the shoe fits…"

I flipped him the bird.

The waitress brought us some water and menus. I ordered both a bloody Mary and coffee, not sure which one would be better for the day, but sure, one or the other would work. Thomas ordered the same.

"So, tell me about your shows." I gave him a smile.

He shook his head "Normally your question would prompt me to rattle on about how fabulous I am, but you already know that. So, let's just cut to the chase. You called *me* remember? Now what's going on?"

I started with the easy one, Diana, the staged scene, the book, music, dinner, and the three failed orgasms.

"Let me get this right…she got you to the edge three times and backed off? I'd seriously hurt someone who denied me an orgasm. They are like little bits of life." He held his hands towards heaven before dramatically sighing. "To leave them hanging is just sacrilege."

I rolled my eyes, "Well, it didn't win her any brownie points. In fact, it kind of sealed the deal on my needing to break things off with her."

"I thought you weren't going to have sex."

"It just happened," I shrugged, "Should've, would've, could've. Throes of passion. All that bullshit. I figured why not try it? What's the worst that could happen?"

"Guess you found out." He pointed at me with his pinkie as he sipped his coffee, "So now what?"

"I have to figure out how to break things off with her. I'm worried she wants to go exclusive. I just don't want her to think it's because the sex sucked."

"Too late for that."

The waitress returned for our order. I went with the Market Omelet; Thomas ordered the Brioche French Toast. Outside the gray skies rolled and a light rain blew in sideways, streaking the windows.

"She asked me out for this coming Saturday, I told her I had plans."

"Liar."

"I know, but she isn't even the biggest issue." I sighed and dug my phone out, pulling up the messages from Secret and passed them over, "This is my real problem. Diana is an irritation. This one on the other hand is getting dangerous." I savored my bloody Mary while he read.

"You have to report her."

"It's just words."

"Words can become actions." Thomas handed the phone back, "I thought you weren't talking to her."

"She came back, last week. Fucking bitch knocked on my door. I thought it might be you and opened it. Secret walked past me, made up some story about losing her phone and how she had to get a new one and replace everyone's numbers."

"So, it took her what, four months to come get your number?"

"I know right?"

"What a freak," he shook his head, "Go on."

"Okay, so she walked in the door, went on about her phone. I knew she was lying. I knew she had something else up her sleeve, so I listened and waited."

The scene played like a movie reel in my mind, how she had been pacing back and forth as she told her lame story.

****

I gave her my number, watched her enter it and poured myself a shot of whiskey. I didn't offer her anything. At last, she stopped moving and faced me.

"I broke up with my girlfriend," she said.

I hadn't expected that. The word girlfriend circled in my mind like a vulture searching for something to tear apart. I took a sip of the whiskey to steady myself, and set it down without shaking, "Girlfriend," I repeated, "How long were you going out?"

"Does it matter?" She batted her eyes at me and

drooped her shoulders down.

No, not really, but yes, yes it mattered because she was here, with some crappy story about losing her phone and needing to get my number. We were basically broken up so why was she telling me this crap now? Why was she here in my place bringing pain back to my life? Why the hell had I let her in?

"Yes." The hurt part of me replied, "It does matter. I deserve to know."

She looked down and a lock of hair hid her eyes, "Since Disneyland."

It made sense. Right after she got back was when she distanced herself and said the dreaded let's be friends. But I wasn't convinced.

"You met her at Disneyland?"

"Yes," she turned away, trailing a finger across the row of books on my window ledge.

"So, she's not from here."

"No, she's from California. We met there and started dating so I broke things off with you when she moved back here with me."

"How old is she?"

"Twenty-two."

"And you live together?"

"We moved here after school—"

"School?"

She wasn't making any sense. I held up a hand and tried to puzzle her story out. It was like a mass of necklaces all tangled together and I didn't know which chain to start with.

"Let me get this right, you moved here together after school?" I was confused, hadn't she just said the "girlfriend" moved out after the trip to California? "I thought you said she *just* moved out here."

Secret flipped her hair out of her eyes with one hand, "No, we met up again in California and she moved back."

"Moved back?" I wrinkled my brow trying to figure it out. Was she talking about the roommate? The reason I had never been over to her place?

"Yes."

"But you said you met her in Disneyland." Lie number one.

"No," she flung her hands up, "We met up again at Disneyland."

"So, she is an old high school friend?" I wanted clarification.

"Yes, from Vegas."

"You said she was from California." Lie number two.

"Does it matter where she's from? I broke up with her." She crossed her arms and looked down at the ground.

I walked away from her. If I had the story right, Secret moved to Seattle after high school with a girlfriend. They got a place together. Her girlfriend was twenty-two. But wait…if she was twenty-two and Secret was twenty-one, then she would have graduated three years ago, which was definitely not last year. Her story was off. It was making my head spin. I rubbed my forehead and turned back to face her.

"Why are you here?"

"I broke my phone last night when I threw it at her and got a new one. I wanted to get your number so maybe…" she looked up at me with big doe eyes, "maybe you could forgive me and take me back."

"You broke your phone." I repeated and it was lie number three.

I don't like being lied to. First, she said she lost her phone, now she broke it. Second, she said she met the girlfriend at Disneyland now it was in high school. Third, she said the girlfriend was from California but changed it to Vegas. The lies were all untangled. My ego and pride were hurt, wounded. My heart was stomping around in its little tower screaming what the fuck! Trust was standing in the corner with her arms crossed saying "I told you so, I told you so…" over and over.

"Get out." I wanted her out, gone, far away from me. I was already wishing I had not given her my number or let her in the door or listened to her. What was that quote about curiosity? Didn't matter…

"But Georgia," she reached for me, and I stepped away from her.

"Don't touch me. You're a fucking liar."

"No, I swear—"

"You had a girlfriend the whole time we were together!"

"No! We were just friends!"

"Did you sleep with her?"

She turned away from me, hands on her hips, and shook her head, "Yes."

"When?" I could feel the anger in me building, growing, firing up.

"Does it matter?" She faced me, wiping at her eyes.

"Yes."

"We had sex once."

"You said you never had sex with a woman." Oh my God and it was lie number four coming down the tracks, roaring with lightening! What the hell! "This whole thing has been nothing but a game to you!" I was seeing red now, explosive, volcanic red.

"No-no, I love you."

She put a hand on my shoulder, and I flung it off. She was incapable of love. I pointed to the door, "Get out of my house." My voice was a steel-edged blade.

She stood for a moment, stunned, speechless, head cocked to the right like she was trying to puzzle things out. Clearly, she hadn't expected me to turn her down. Her hands were still outstretched, waiting, and then they dropped to her side. She opened her mouth to say something, and I shouted, "NOW!"

It was like a slap. She flinched, but recovered, her hands clenched into fists, her shoulders straightened, and her eyes narrowed into knives. The air was taut, like a stretched wire before it broke.

"You'll be sorry for this," she hissed as she passed me.

"I'm sorry I ever let you in my life," I replied.

There was an icy rage in her eyes as she glared back at me. I met her fury with my own and shot it down. She slammed the door. I didn't care.

****

The scene faded like a bad dream, and I waved for another drink. "She slammed the door and that was that."

"Psycho." Thomas rolled his eyes, "So, what are you going to do?"

"Nothing," I shrugged, the messages told a good story, but they were just words. I didn't know her real name, I didn't have any photos of her, and even the cops would say I had nothing to go on. I was screwed. "I'm going to write about her." I nodded, "I have this story I'm working on, and she will be my villain."

"You're writing? Am I in it?" Thomas clapped his hands together.

"Yes," I replied to both questions.

"Who is the main character?"

"I'm still trying to figure his name out, he looks like the barista at Secrets named Todd, but he is mysterious like this guy who comes in wearing a trench coat. He is going through a bad divorce, meets this woman but is harboring a secret..." Talking about my story idea already made me feel lighter.

"And your villainess?" Thomas air quoted the last word.

"Oh, get this! Looks wise she is based on this hot looking blonde I almost ran into, but she is the main characters ex, an evil, manipulative, narcissistic bitch I am going to base on everyone—including the psycho Secret I mistakenly dated. I am going to payback all of them with her death. Vengeance via the power of the pen." I smiled, a wicked delicious grin.

"Damn girl, do I at least get a happy ending?"

"You will be the reigning queen of the west coast and will save the hero, fall in love, and live happily ever after." I raised my glass, "Now, enough of my crap, distract me with your life, Thomas."

"Oh, you know me," he waved a manicured hand, "I'm still searching for Mr. Right, but last night I met the sweetest young thing..."

I listened to him prattle on through the rest of brunch. Who knew, he might have something I could use in my story.

"Promise to call me when you get home?" Thomas asked as we paid the bill.

"I promise." I replied.

I huddled into my coat, gave him a hug at the door, and we went our separate ways. It was a deceiving day. The rain had slowed to a slicing drizzle. Seagulls hovered, surfing the breeze, floating with wings stretched out. I felt the crowd of Sunday gathering and checked my phone, surprised to not see a text. Part of me wondered why, the other part was relieved. It hit me that much as I had managed to get over Secret and move on, somehow she'd crept back into my life, unbidden, unwanted, and now threatening. She was like an itch I couldn't scratch, an annoying and persistent mosquito I couldn't swat. I was tired of looking over my shoulder. I was tired of worry wrapping its fingers around me, clutching me tight. My gut told me her threats were as harmless and useless as her words of love had been. She was all talk, all crap, all bullshit, and I wanted her out of my head. She was not what I wanted to focus on. I had better things to think of, like the characters in my story and the way it was coming together, like my job which was moving into the suck the life out of everything Holiday Season.

I drifted with the crowd past the booths in the Market, checking out all the unique treasures one could find. They ranged anywhere from wine glass flattened trays, to animal figurines created from Mount Saint Helens volcanic ash. I fingered one of the glass wind chimes, tried some of the honey lotion, and threw a couple dollars in the street vendors guitar case.

The sounds of the market belonged on a music station. The heartbeat and pulse of Pikes Place reminded me of why I fell for Seattle in the first place, why I had wanted to move here, walk the streets and rediscover myself. My problem was I was still in hiding, still locked away in a tower of solitary confinement which would explain why I picked losers to date, including the cherry on the top "Secret" who wouldn't go out in public with me. I needed to get out of my tower; The key was my story, the door was Seattle.

I wanted my love for Seattle to shine through on the page. I wanted Seattle to almost seem to be one of the characters, the strong one in the background always there for the main character to fall back on, turn to. I wanted to paint my love for Seattle in drops of words. Which meant I needed to include everything I loved about the city, including her dark underbelly.

I stopped at one of the vegetable vendors and picked up a purple and red mottled Cherokee tomato, a Walla Walla onion, and a plump orange pepper. I handed them to the vendor along with some green beans. The next vendor talked me into a trying an Autumn Glory apple which tasted like honey and cinnamon. I bought some strange, tiny eggplant looking grapes as well.

"These are moon drop grapes," The vendor said.

They tasted like what I imagined the color purple would: rich, exotic, and sweet. I stopped at one of the fish mongers, adding some fresh clams, scallops, shrimp, and a salmon fillet to my purchases. The best seafood and fish could always be found at Pikes Place.

There was so much life in Seattle to embrace. I needed to get out more, broaden my horizons, meet new people, join some groups, and get involved in my life. I had a lot to live for.

Walking home, I deliberately refused to glance over my shoulder or at the people I passed. Letting myself into my apartment, my tower, my solitary confinement, I locked the door and plugged my lights in. I texted

Thomas, let him know I had made it home safe, and turned my music on. Kicking off my shoes I danced into the main room and put the groceries away. I plopped a moon drop grape in my mouth, poured myself a glass of wine, and started creating dinner. This was my life. This was what I was used to. I enjoyed my solitude. Maybe that was why no one could enter my tower? I enjoyed being on my own with no one to answer to. Swaying to the beat, I sauteed a mix of veggies and seafood, topped my wine off, and made myself a plate.

The rain had stopped and the sun was setting in a curtain dropping flame, seeming to almost melt into the bay, its reflection like dripped wax. I turned my computer on, read over my last few lines, and corrected a couple spots. The story was coming along well, I felt it was a good beginning, kind of like an appetizer, only the characters were being served up instead of food.

I had left off with my main character meeting the woman his evil ex set him up with. The woman was a trap. After talking to Thomas, I wondered if maybe my main character should be closeted and secretly in love with a drag queen? Hmmm…it could be an interesting twist. I went back through the scene, changed a few things, and started to write. The words were flowing, the story was spilling onto the page, and everything was coming together, when my phone dinged.

Probably Thomas. Sighing, I got up, set my plate in the sink, and thumbed the phone to life. One message. Secret, not Thomas.

—*You think you can just ignore me? Treat me like I am nothing? You'll pay for that. You better watch your back*—

I read the message again. I should watch my back?

I was so done with the "what if's" she was planting in my mind, so done with her empty threats and words. I set the phone down, walked away, went back, and picked it up. What the hell was her problem? Was she out there right now? Was she watching me? She would have to have binoculars to see me. Would she try anything physical? The phone dinged again.

—I'm not done with you—

I'm not done with you? What did that mean? God she was a mess. A viper. A mistake. I wanted nothing to do with her. I wanted to forget her, erase her, and kill her off in my story. The story was my salvation, the words my bridge to a dream. I could write and heal and with the words I would make it through the upcoming chaos of the Holidays. I needed the words, needed the feel of the keys, and the whispering of the muse. I didn't need her bullshit and empty threats.

Another message dinged.

I didn't want to look at it, but...damn curiosity. It was a picture of a hand holding a large knife. What the hell was that about? Was she threatening to stab me? Seriously? But the angle was wrong, it looked more like she was threatening to stab herself and how did that make sense? *I'm not done with you,* followed by a picture of a knife against her wrist. I didn't get it and frankly, I didn't care. She could take her fucked up game and shove it. I was done with her bullshit. I clicked on her messages and saved them to a file labeled "Shh...don't answer."

"Well, I'm done with you," I said out loud, sipped my wine, and blocked her number. She wasn't worth a reply.

And that...was where I made my mistake.

A word about the author...

Raised in the desert heat of southern Utah, Gina escaped to Washington State for twenty-three wonderful years. She fell in love with the evergreen trees, gray cloudy mornings, rain and the city of Seattle. Family and personal reasons brought a return to the desert with its endless summers and coral canyons. Every day she misses the rain. She is a member of the League of Utah Writers, has received a second-place award for Prose and was a finalist for the southern Utah Poetry Slam team. Her short stories have been published in a local magazine.

Secrets Cafe is her first novel, written as a love letter to the city of Seattle and to all her friends who still live there.